WHERE THE
DEER AND THE
ANTELOPE PLAY

Crossway Books by
STEPHEN BLY

THE STUART BRANNON WESTERN SERIES

Hard Winter at Broken Arrow Crossing
False Claims at the Little Stephen Mine
Last Hanging at Paradise Meadow
Standoff at Sunrise Creek
Final Justice at Adobe Wells
Son of an Arizona Legend

THE CODE OF THE WEST SERIES

It's Your Misfortune and None of My Own
One Went to Denver and the Other Went Wrong
Where the Deer and the Antelope Play

THE NATHAN T. RIGGINS WESTERN ADVENTURE SERIES
(AGES 9–14)

The Dog Who Would Not Smile
Coyote True
You Can Always Trust a Spotted Horse
The Last Stubborn Buffalo in Nevada
Never Dance with a Bobcat
Hawks Don't Say Goodbye

THE AUSTIN-STONER FILES

The Lost Manuscript of Martin Taylor Harrison

CODE OF THE WEST
BOOK THREE

WHERE THE DEER AND THE ANTELOPE PLAY

Stephen Bly

CROSSWAY BOOKS • WHEATON, ILLINOIS
A DIVISION OF GOOD NEWS PUBLISHERS

Library of Congress Cataloging-in-Publication Data
Bly, Stephen A., 1944-
  Where the deer and the antelope play / Stephen Bly.
    p.   cm.—(Code of the West; bk. 3)
    I. Title   II. Series: Bly, Stephen A., 1944- Code of the West: bk. 3.
PS3552.L93W48 1995   813'.54—dc20   95-14510
ISBN 0-89107-850-9 *5,39/8.99 Ingram*

04	03	02	01	00	99	98	97	96	95
15	14	13	12	11	10	9	8	7	6	5	4	3	2	1

40151   7-1-98

FOR
ANNE CHONKO
MY TRAIL PARTNER
IN
MARTINSBURG, PENNSYLVANIA

1

Wade Eagleman smoked a large, loosely rolled cigar as he reclined in the leather-backed captain's chair on the other side of the poker table. With long, black hair and Comanche heritage, he exuded confidence.

The man at the right of Tap Andrews sported a flopping, dirty gray hat and tobacco-stained vest. The blank expression on his face revealed either the coldness of a seasoned gambler or the stare of ignorance.

The fat-faced man on the left was dressed well—frock coat, silk tie, and top hat. Sweat beaded on his forehead as he nervously rapped his empty whiskey glass on the scarred, unfinished wooden table.

"Cards?" Eagleman asked. "Tap, how many do you want?"

"What? Oh . . . yeah. Well . . ." He slid open the unindexed playing cards slowly and watched each one come into view.

Ace of clubs.

Nine of hearts.

Eight of spades.

Eight of clubs.

Ace of spades.

Black aces and eights!

"Come on, Tap, it's gettin' close to noon. How many cards do you want?"

With the thick cloud of tobacco smoke hovering over the table and burning his eyes, Tap looked up at Eagleman. "What time is it?"

"Eleven thirty."

"I'm dead!"

Eagleman pulled the cigar out of his mouth. "The hand can't be that bad."

"The wedding!" Tap shouted, throwing his cards faceup on the table. "I've got to get to the wedding by noon!"

"I thought you said that ranch of yours was three or four days from here."

"I'm goin' to be late!" Tap jumped up and felt the frigid floor press against his bare feet. "Where'd I put my horse? Is Brownie out front?"

"You can't make it. It's all over, Mr. Tapadera Andrews!" Suddenly a sweet-smelling woman slipped her arm around his waist and hugged him tight.

"Rena? What are you doin' here?"

Her raven hair hung down in curls past her shoulders. Her full lips pouted with each word, and her purple dress had carelessly slipped off her left shoulder. "Sugar, why don't you give up on that yellow-haired siren and come back home to me?" she cooed.

"I've got to get to the wedding. I've got to go."

"You ain't goin' nowhere, Andrews!" the man with the floppy hat announced, whipping out his revolver and pointing it at Tap's head. "Nobody skips out of a game when Eddie Chase is losin'! Sit down!"

"Look, Chase . . . you can have the pot. I don't want it. I've got to ride out to the ranch. Why am I sitting here without my boots on?"

The flying chair blindsided him, and Tap crumpled to the floor as the oak wood splintered above him. He rolled under a table just as a loud explosion ripped lead into the floor next to him and filled the room with gun smoke. He yanked his .44, cocked the hammer, and aimed at the man shooting wildly.

Just as Tap pulled the trigger, everything went dark.

Very dark.

And cold.

December 1882, Triple Creek Ranch, Larimer County, Colorado.

The rough wool blanket grated the stubble of his unshaven face as Tap Andrews tried to hide from the black predawn cold. His left foot felt icy as he slid it back under the covers across the worn flannel sheets. He buried his hands under the lumpy pillow and let his mind drift to warmer nights.

It's the same dream. Always the same dream.

I'm always late for the wedding. And always cold.

Fumbling for a match, Andrews struggled to light the small lantern next to his rough-cut wood-framed bed and swung his feet to the floor. The wick needed trimming, and the glow from the lamp barely illuminated the bedroom that was decorated with several piles of dirty clothes. The wood beneath his bare feet felt smooth, hard, and cold. The stampede string flopped down the back of his neck as he jammed on the gray felt hat and staggered toward the doorway to the living room.

Clothed in long-handled underwear, Tap carried the lantern in one hand and the matches in the other. His left foot didn't make it through the doorway. He came to an abrupt halt when he slammed it into the half-open door.

Andrews dropped the matches, hopped into the large living room, and clutched at his throbbing toes. In the glimmer of the flickering lantern, he spotted a gray and white fur ball on the floor next to the hearth.

"Sal, you lazy mouser, you let the fire go out! How many times have I told you to toss another stick on those coals?"

The cat opened one yellow-green eye, then quickly closed it.

Tap scooped up the matches, hunkered down in front of the large rock fireplace, and quickly built a fire. The pine crackled and snapped, producing a little warmth as he rubbed his freezing toes.

He packed the lantern back into the bedroom and then sat on the edge of the bed to tug on socks that felt dirty. The worn brown boots were cold as he yanked them on and stood up. His left toes still throbbed. He felt stiffness in his right shoulder and a cramp just below his right rib cage.

They can take out the bullets and the knife blades, but they can't take the hurt away. A man lives with old wounds forever, don't he, Lord?

Wearing hat, boots, and long johns, Andrews shuffled out to the kitchen and sorted through a pile of dirty tin dishes.

I thought I was goin' to wash these up last night. Oh, yeah. I got cold rebuildin' that saddle. Maybe if it warms up this afternoon . . .

He grabbed a blue enameled coffeepot, opened the lid, held the lantern above his head, and peered inside.

"It'll do another day." He reached into a brown cloth sack hidden among the pots and pans and scooped up a handful of coffee. "I'll just water this down a little and boil it up."

Tap broke the thin crust of ice across the top of the water pitcher with his fingers. Then he scooted back into the living room and hung the coffeepot on a hook above the roaring fire. Stepping to the bedroom, he retrieved a wool blanket from the bed, returned to the fire, and wrapped the blanket around himself.

He stood there, toasting first one side and then the other, until he heard the water in the pot boiling. The liquid that coursed into the tin cup looked gritty and black. It tasted bitter and hot. Finally, he dragged the wooden rocking chair up by the fire and sat down, letting the heat from the cup warm his hands. He shoved his hat to the back of his head and sipped the steaming drink.

Warmed on the outside by the blanket and the fire and on the inside by boiled coffee, he closed his eyes and let the tin cup dangle from his fingers.

I'll need to clean this place up before the weddin'. Good thing Pepper's not coming out till next week. Maybe I could just leave it for her . . . and I'm not goin' to wear that ruffled-front shirt no matter how many times she bats those purdy green eyes. . . . Oh, Pepper, I wish . . . it's like a little kid waitin' for Christmas. Only better.

The sound of hoof beats on frozen ground brought him out of his sleep. Tap strapped his Colt .44 onto his long johns before his eyes had time to focus in the breaking light of early dawn.

"Tap, it's me—Wiley. From the Rafter R!" The shout filtered through the heavy wooden front door.

Andrews swung open the door and stepped out onto the porch. The rider's horse blew steam and pranced in the front yard.

"Put your pony in the barn and come get some hot coffee," Tap greeted him. "I wasn't expectin' company this early."

"I sort of assumed that by your costume," Wiley joshed.

Andrews noticed the frost on Wiley's eyebrows and beard. "On second thought, go get that coffee. I'll put the horse in the barn."

"This is one time I'll take you up on that."

"You been ridin' all night?"

"Yep."

"Well, scout out a clean cup in the kitchen and warm up by the fire. I'll be right back."

Andrews led the horse to the barn, hurriedly pulled off the tack, and stalled the animal with some fresh hay next to Brownie. His hands were numb and aching by the time he hustled back.

Wiley hunched down by the fire with a cup of coffee in his hand, his brown hat hung on his back. His short, dark hair showed only a slight sign of hat curl.

"That's the first time I've seen long-handled underwear turn purple in the cold." Wiley laughed.

"Well, if you're just goin' to gripe all day, I might as well get dressed!" Tap stepped into the bedroom and yanked off his boots. "What in the world are you doin' out at night in this kind of weather?" he shouted to the man in the other room.

"Lookin' for a job. You got any winter work?"

Tap pulled a wool shirt over his head. "Work? What happened with you and Fightin' Ed?"

"I quit!"

"When?" Tap buttoned his ducking trousers and yanked the suspenders up over his shoulders. Carrying his boots back into the front room, he plopped down at the bench next to the grand piano.

"Last night at sundown. Me and Fightin' Ed had a slight disagreement." Tap noticed Wiley was clean shaven except for the sloping sideburns.

"It must have been some row. Quittin' a winter job is mighty risky."

"Well, Fightin' Ed's been losin' some cattle on the south range this winter. Yesterday we tracked the rustlers to the state line."

"On my place?"

"Probably right along the base of the Medicine Bows. Fightin' Ed's convinced that you're either stealin' cows or harborin' some rustlers. He'll be comin' down to pay you a visit either tonight or tomorrow."

"And you rode all night to warn me?"

"Shoot, no. I rode all night lookin' for a job."

"Well, I got a little woodstove in the tack room in the barn. You can bunk there and share some grub, but I can't pay you anything. It'll give you a place to winter out."

"I might take you up on it for a week or two. Don't figure to stay in this cold too long. 'Course, if Fightin' Ed has his way, neither of us will be around."

"If someone's rustlin' cattle, I'll help him catch 'em."

"Tap, Fightin' Ed is goin' to use this as an excuse to chase you out of the country."

"I don't chase."

"Yeah. That's why I decided to pull stakes and drift. I don't intend on being in the long-range sights of your .44-40."

Tap felt a shiver slide down his back, and he moved closer to the fire. "A little help is always welcome. But I'm goin' to have to settle this quick. I'm gettin' married on the 22nd."

"I'll light shuck before then. I've got kinfolk down in New Mexico. Thought I'd slide down there for Christmas."

"I didn't aim to shuffle you off."

"Tap, a man deserves a little peace and privacy on his weddin'—that's for sure . . . that is, if Fightin' Ed lets you live that long. You marryin' that blonde-haired girl down at McCurleys'?"

"Yep."

"She ain't got no sisters, has she? I mean, I could stick around for the weddin' at least."

Tap laughed and stirred up the fire with another log. "No sisters, but there just might be a purdy girl or two stop by. We're havin' it here at the ranch. Just a few friends and the preacher. You're certainly invited."

"I ain't got no foofaraw outfit to wear."

"That's no problem. You like those shirts with ruffles?"

"What?"

"Eh—nothin'. How 'bout some breakfast, Wiley?"

Tap scrounged the kitchen for a couple of clean plates, and within a half hour had them piled with steaming fried eggs, salt pork, and leftover sourdough biscuits. He and Wiley shoved aside the saddle being repaired on the dining table and sat down to eat.

"The bigger the place, the bigger the mess." Tap shrugged as he waved his arms around the living room.

"You lookin' forward to havin' a permanent housekeeper, I suppose."

"That's one of many advantages!" Tap grinned. "I was supposed to clean this place up for Pepper's visit, but she's helpin' out the McCurleys and won't be ridin' out this week."

"So there ain't no need to tidy up?"

"Nah. But I might just take a bath anyway. You think Fightin' Ed will be crossin' the border this mornin' or tonight?"

"I'd guess it would take him most of the day to get some supplies and gather the crew."

"It doesn't make much sense for a rustler to push cattle south into the mountains. If I were them, I'd head east to Cheyenne."

"Or north to the goldfields in Montana."

"Exactly. Anyway, I think I'll go scout out my place before the Rafter R boys swamp me. Maybe I can cut a trail and figure this thing out before Fightin' Ed causes a ruckus."

"I'll ride with ya," Wiley volunteered.

"Appreciate the thought, but you look like a buffalo drug you through a blizzard. Scoot up there and keep my fire goin'. Take a little siesta. There's a blanket in that rockin' chair. It can be mighty peaceful out here—unless you rock back on that cat's tail. That makes him so mad he won't talk to ya for a week."

"Thanks, Tap. My bones are frozen. But I'm standin' with ya when the Rafter R boys show. Not a one of them will take a shot at me except maybe Drew Blackstone."

"And Fightin' Ed."

"Oh, yeah. Fightin' Ed would shoot his own mother when he gets mad."

"I don't think this is a shootin' matter. I'll be happy to help him catch rustlers—and all I have on this ranch are those longhorns he didn't want."

"He sure wanted to buy this place, you know."

"Well . . . I'm goin' to have a look around. I don't think there's more than a foot of snow anywhere but in the drifts. I'll be back in a couple hours. That ought to give me plenty of time to figure out how to handle the Rafter R boys."

The barn was icy . . . the leather stiff . . . and Brownie sullied about, not looking forward to leaving his stall. With worn deer-skin gloves, Tap saddled and cinched the gelding. He pulled down some hay for the other horses and broke the ice off the water trough.

Yanking his hat down tight, he turned the collar up on his coat and mounted the horse. The saddle was frigid, and the ducking trousers taut as he rode north of the barn. Neither the stubbled beard nor the callous Colorado morning could hide the tanned skin of his mother's Métis heritage.

Daylight streaked the sky over the snow-clad Medicine Bows to the east. The creeks had frozen weeks before and were now only ribbons of ice lacing through cottonwood skeletons. Some tufts of brown grass jutted out of the snow beds of the little valley.

The low, rolling hills of the west were smooth—like white, icy sand dunes. Only an occasional sagebrush broke the view. No clouds coursed the sky, but a purple morning tint signaled that the temperature would stay below freezing no matter how bright the sun.

The arctic air rolling against his face bordered on pain. Tap felt chilled to the bone before he lost sight of the barn. He pulled his ragged burgundy bandanna up over his nose to warm the air that entered his lungs.

It's a good day for stayin' next to the fire and fixin' up that old saddle. Who in the world would want to go out and rustle cattle on a day like this?

Tap pulled his Winchester '73 from the scabbard and shoved in several more cartridges from his bullet belt before putting it away. He yanked his Colt and spun the chamber, then let it slip back into the Mexican double-loop holster.

His toes were numb. He remembered how old-timers wrapped their boots with flour sacks and crammed them into the tapaderas.

Pride. That's all that keeps me from doin' it. I wonder how many proud men have frozen to death?

The only sound was the steady crunch as the standard bay gelding broke through the snow crust with each step. It was a steady, plodding rhythm that caused a man to drift off in thought . . . fall asleep . . . or both.

Lord, I really don't need a hassle from the Rafter R or from rustlers for the next few weeks. I've been hanging out at the ranch ever since that ruckus with Dillard and Barranca in Denver. Shoot, I've only been to April's once and McCurleys' four times. I don't aim to do anything to upset things now.

A quiet winter.

A quiet wedding.

Maybe I'll ride into McCurleys' in the mornin'. Hate to wait 'til Sunday to see Pepper.

The bawl of a cow disrupted his thoughts, and he instantly struck Brownie with his spurs and trotted towards the sound. Tap crested a rise in the valley floor and looked across at the small herd of cattle munching on what brown grass towered above the snow.

"What?" he choked.

Scattered among the speckled and blotched longhorns were several white-faced Herefords.

"Rafter R—no doubt! Brownie, what in the world are these cows doin' in my herd? I mean, besides catching Spanish fever?"

He trotted past the herd and followed their tracks back up the valley. Near Warm Springs he found where the Rafter R cattle had been driven down from the mountains and mixed with the others. In the crushed snow he found four sets of hoofprints.

They brought them down here and then turned around and went back to the high line.

Within half an hour he was riding the first row of piñon pines and scrub cedars on the front edge of the Medicine Bow Mountains. Four horses in crusty snow left an easy trail to follow.

Either they want someone to follow them, or they have no idea in the world that anyone would be out here.

Tap pulled the Winchester, cocked it, thumbed the hammer back until it clicked once, and laid the weapon across his lap. Brownie twitched his nose and lifted his head, causing Tap to rein up and stare through the trees.

What do you smell, boy? Another pony? A fire? Where are they?

He rubbed the horse's neck and studied the tree-scattered horizon.

There's no way to sneak up on anyone in this snow. It's like havin' a military band lead the way.

He rode Brownie up to a stand of scrub cedars and dismounted.

"There's smoke up there somewhere, isn't there, boy?"

Tying the horse to a tree limb, he released the two bottom buttons of his coat and pulled the rifle from the scabbard.

"You wait for me. Just think about warm barns and fresh hay. I'll take a little peek and see who these men are."

Tap shoved the bandanna back down around his neck and hiked higher up on the mountainside. His legs felt stiff. His toes throbbed. The bones in his fingers ached as they clutched the hardened-steel receiver of the rifle. The air burned his lungs, but it was the bitter taste that caught his attention.

Smoke! If you can't see it or smell it, you can taste it!

The snow around the trees was softer, and he quietly crept from trunk to trunk searching for some sign of the rustlers. About the time his boots were beginning to feel like blocks of ice, he spotted shadowy movements below him in a clearing. Descending behind the cedars and pines, Tap sighted the small, hot-burning fire and several figures huddled around it. On the far side were four unsaddled horses tied off to a rope that had been stretched between two trees.

They don't plan on havin' to leave in a hurry. Four horses, three men. Someone's missin'. Or maybe one's a pack horse. If they aim on runnin' those cows south, they'll need a packhorse. But those tracks sure didn't look like one of those ponies was bein' led.

He inched closer, continually scanning the scattered trees around the fire.

Where's that fourth man? Come on, you can't stay away from the fire for too long. Where'd you drift off to?

Andrews held the rifle in the crook of his arm and tugged off his gloves. Blowing hot breath into his hands, he rubbed them together, then drew his Colt, and shoved a bullet from his belt into the one empty chamber. He holstered his revolver and blew on his hands again before pulling on the stiff leather gloves.

Tap stared for several minutes at the dancing yellow flames of the fire. A cold breeze caught the back of his neck and shivered all the way to the base of his spine.

If there's only three of them, I could be waitin' out here all day!

Andrews had decided to go ahead and move in on the trio when he saw movement on the other side of the horses.

There he is!

"It's about time, Karl. We was thinkin' you done got lost!"

The voices were distant but distinct in the silence of the mountain. With rifle pointed toward the flames, Tap crept closer to the men.

"You reckon them longhorns will bring as much as the white faces?"

"A beefsteak's a beefsteak. Them miners don't care what they eat."

"Well, we better get on the trail. If we ever get a first-class snow, we won't reach Rico Springs until May."

Rico Springs?

"I'll tell you all one thing—when we get the money for this batch, I'm headed straight for that dance hall at Pingree Hill. Them girls at April's could warm a dead man's blood."

The big man called Karl circled the fire. "That Rafter R crew will be ridin' down here soon. Let's throw them back on the trail and get out of here."

"They ain't never followed us into Colorado before."

"Let 'em come," a blanket-covered man boasted. "Them drovers will hightail it back home as soon as a little lead starts flyin'."

They never met Fightin' Ed Casey, I presume.

"You three goin' to squat there like grass widows at the box social, or are we goin' to move some cattle?"

A man with a wide black hat and blond beard jumped to his feet waving a revolver. "Who you callin' a grass wida?" he shouted.

The clinched fist of the big man caught the gun-waving man on the chin and sent him sprawling into the snow next to the fire.

"Don't you ever, ever draw that gun on me, boy!"

The man in the snow sat up slowly, rubbing his chin and recovering his revolver.

"You do that again, Karl, and I'll . . ."

If I had time, I'd just let you kill each other, Tap thought.

He pulled the glove off his right hand and lifted his Colt from the holster. Carrying the cocked .44 in his right hand and the rifle in his left, he approached the fire.

His voice boomed through the cold mountain air. "If you men will just sit right there for a minute, I think we need to talk about some cattle. Now don't go pullin' guns!"

The startled men spun toward him, and the blond-bearded one pointed his revolver toward Tap, cocked the hammer, and began to squeeze the trigger.

Andrews fired his .44, striking the man in the right leg halfway between the knee and the hip.

"He shot me!" the man cried, dropping his gun and clutching his leg.

"Leave 'em holstered, boys. My next shot won't be for the leg!"

"I told you the Rafter R drovers would follow us down here!"

"Karl, how many do you see? Are they back in the trees?"

"You done shot Jimmy Ray!"

Andrews watched their eyes as the other three men searched the mountainside behind him. "That's one of the chances he took when he tried to kill me."

"Help me, Karl . . . I'm bleedin' bad!"

Stepping closer to the three, Andrews nodded. "You better tie a bandanna around that leg. But in this cold, it's a wonder the blood will flow at all."

One of the men stood with a blanket still around his shoulders and stepped toward Jimmy Ray. Ducking under the aim of the revolver, he lunged for Andrews's feet.

Instead, he ran headlong into the swinging barrel of the .44-40 rifle, and the man sank to his knees. Blood from his forehead dripped on the clean, white snow. Tap swung the barrel of the Winchester again and jammed it into the stomach of the big man just as he was lifting his revolver.

"Unless you four plan on dyin' right here, I suggest we talk a spell first."

"You're a dead man, mister. You can't take all four of us," the one remaining at the fire growled.

"Two are down, and if I twitch my finger even the slightest, old Karl here is gut-shot. That just leaves you and me. Now I haven't ever seen you draw, but you've seen what I can do to your friends, so you want to try it? Just nod and go for your gun."

"Wait!" Karl shouted. "We can talk."

"I'm dyin', Karl," Jimmy Ray cried. "Shoot the—"

"You ain't dyin'! Not yet anyway," Karl shouted. "Help the boys, Hank. And leave that gun holstered 'til we sort this out. Now back that .44 away from my gut, mister, and let's talk."

While the one called Hank helped the other two tie bandages, Tap backed off but kept the Winchester in his left hand and the Colt in his right.

"You ain't from the Rafter R?" Karl questioned.

"Nope."

"You by yourself?"

"Now that's somethin' I reckon you four will just have to ponder."

"If you ain't Rafter R, what are you doin' up here in the middle of winter?"

"I own this ranch."

"What ranch?"

"The Triple Creek. Don't you know where you are?"

"Ranch? This is open land!"

"Nope. And those longhorns belong to me."

"Longhorns have been runnin' wild in these mountains for years. They don't belong to nobody!"

"The ones with the TC brand belong to me."

"Brand? We didn't see no brand," the one with the bleeding forehead declared.

"Mister, you can't get us for rustlin' your cows 'cause we haven't touched 'em yet," Karl protested.

"That's right!" Jimmy Ray cried. "And those others came from Wyomin'."

"Look, mister, we'll saddle up and take our Herefords on south. We won't cut out any of those longhorns, I swear. You can flip up that long-range peep sight and lead down the first one of us that gathers your calves."

"Boys, those Herefords don't belong to you. But I will give you a choice. You can either round them up and push 'em right back up to the Rafter R and take your chances with Fightin' Ed Casey, or you can mount up and head for Denver and let me take those cows home."

"You ain't goin' to steal our cows!" Hank defied him.

"Well, there is another choice. I can just shoot you right here and let the buzzards pick your bones clean."

"I'm a hurtin' real bad, Karl," Jimmy Ray cried. "I need a doctor."

"We can take him, Karl!"

"Hank . . . he's got that Winchester pointed at my belly, not yours. There's no question we could kill him, but I don't aim to take a bullet just to prove that."

Andrews looked the big man over. "You're a smarter man than I figured you for, Karl."

"I expect we'll meet again sometime, mister," Karl growled. "I hope you'll be packin' a gun then too."

"I reckon I will be."

"Come on, boys, let's saddle up."

"We ain't goin' to jist leave him with our cows, are we?"

"Jimmy Ray, you're lucky I don't just leave you lyin' in the snow."

Tap stood across from the fire and watched them saddle their horses and load their gear. The barrel of his revolver followed Karl's every movement. By the time they were ready to ride, he had stirred the fire into a blaze.

"Mister, I'll be gettin' even with you!" Jimmy Ray threatened. "You better be lookin' over your shoulder!"

Andrews shook his head. "Karl, get him out of here before I shoot him again!"

"What's your name, mister? I want to know who I'm gunnin' fer," Jimmy Ray cried.

"Tap Andrews."

"The one that took on Jordan Beckett and Victor Barranca?"

"I had some help."

"Barranca shot a friend of ours in the back."

"He shot a lot of men in the back."

"Yeah . . . well, how about you, Andrews? You ever shoot men in the back?"

"Nope."

"That's what I'm countin' on." Karl spurred his tall black horse and galloped south through the snow with the other three trailing behind.

Within minutes Tap had his gun holstered and his gloves off, trying to warm his aching fingers over the flames of the crackling fire.

He finally left the warmth long enough to retrieve Brownie. The saddle was so cold that he stood in the stirrups all the way back to the campfire. Tap pulled the saddle off the horse and plopped it down on a granite rock that he had rolled next to the fire. Then he sat on the gradually warming saddle and gingerly pulled the snow-covered boots off his numb feet.

Propping his feet up as close to the fire as he could, Tap clenched his teeth as the extreme pain of recirculation gripped each foot.

I can't cut them out and hold them by myself. I can't let

Fightin' Ed find 'em grazin' with mine, or he'll think I stole 'em
for sure.
  Nothin's simple.
  Everything's—everything's so . . .
  Cold!
Tap shoved all the remaining wood on the fire. The bright win-
ter sun, even though low on the southern horizon, reflected off the
snow and glared into his furrow-framed eyes. Tap blinked them
shut as he felt the warmth of the fire dance across his face and feet.
His bare hands were stretched out across his knees, his rifle
propped against his saddle. He took a long, deep breath, and for
the first time since he left the ranch, the air didn't burn his lungs.
  I'll just rest here for a minute.
  There's work to be done.
His head dropped to his chest.
This time there was no dream.

  "Well, well, well, looky here! Rustlin' my cattle plumb wore
you out, did it?"
  A painfully cold gun barrel was shoved against his temple. Tap
blinked his eyes open at what was left of the dying campfire.
  "Come on in, men," the gravelly voice next to him shouted.
"We caught him barefoot and nappin'!"
  "Fightin' Ed! What are you doin' here?" Tap managed to
mutter.
  "Chasin' rustlers. And we just caught ourselves a big one!"

2

eads of sweat dashed across Pepper Paige's forehead and flooded the corner of her eye with a salty, stinging regularity. She tried to brush them back with the sleeve of her yellow dress, careful not to streak flour across her face.

The kitchen at McCurley Hotel was stifling. Both cookstoves roared as Mrs. Mac, Margaret, and Lupe scurried to serve an overflow crowd at the dining tables in the next room.

Pepper knew that her blonde hair had long ago escaped from the combs, and she could feel it sticking to the back of her neck. Her feet, bound in the hot lace-up black shoes, ached from the constant standing.

It's like Saturday night at the dance hall! Two more weeks— then you can say goodbye to all of this! I suppose Tap and me will sit in front of the fireplace some nights . . . then again maybe not!

She knew it was more than the heat of the kitchen causing her to blush.

"Pepper, that second oven is empty now. You want me to put in the berry cobbler?"

"Thanks, Mrs. McCurley. Goodness, it's hot in here tonight!"

"You think this is bad? I've got six cigar smokers out there. Why, even one of those despicable dance halls couldn't be any worse than that!"

Mrs. McCurley put her hand over her mouth. "Oh! I didn't mean that to sound personal!"

Pepper wiped her forehead again, this time dusting it with a fine tint of white wheat flour. "I was thinking the same thing." She laughed. "And don't worry about me. I am what I am. If it don't matter to God or Tap what I used to do, well, it surely don't matter to me."

She carried the deep tin baking pan to the cookstove oven and slipped it in with a definitive sigh.

It was almost two hours later when she hung the damp dish towels on the rack in the pantry and pulled off her apron. Mrs. McCurley sat on a chair in the corner of the kitchen, rubbing her now-bare feet.

"Honey, don't ever get old and overweight. It kills your feet!"

"I'm bushed. Think I'll wash up and go to bed," Pepper put in.

"Did you want to talk about that wedding menu?"

"Oh . . . yes, I did make a new list. But I'm too tired now. Are you and Mr. Mac still planning on driving out to the ranch with me tomorrow?"

"Yep. We need the break." Mrs. McCurley's eyes sparkled even when framed by well-seasoned wrinkles. "Most of the guests are going out on the early stage. This might be their last chance to make Denver before Christmas. That pass won't stay open too much longer."

"Well, let's talk about the menu on the way out to the Triple Creek. I told Tap we probably couldn't make it this week, so this visit will surprise him."

Mrs. McCurley sipped hot tea from a chipped porcelain cup. "We sure will miss havin' you around here. If you hadn't volunteered to help us through, we'd have been swamped."

"It's making the time pass more quickly. I'm just glad I don't have to sit around up in my room all day counting the hours."

"You're pretty anxious for that weddin', aren't you?"

"Sometimes I want it to happen so bad I'm afraid that it won't. Do you know what I mean?"

"My memory may be fadin', honey, but I remember my weddin'. I was a nervous wreck."

"But everything came off all right, didn't it? I mean, all that worry was for nothing, right?"

"Well, it came off mighty nice, but not exactly as we planned."

"What happened?"

"The church was awful hot—about as hot as this kitchen, and Robert fainted."

"He what?"

"Yep. Right up in the front of the church standin' next to the preacher."

"What did you do?"

"They poured water on his face, and we said our vows sittin' on the wailin' bench. None of that will happen to you. I've never seen a wedding more organized."

Pepper rubbed her long, thin fingers and noticed how rough her hands were becoming. "Mrs. McCurley, my whole life has been one disorganized mess. In the dance hall we just tripped along from one disaster to another. A fight, a stabbing, some girl crying, some drunk breaking up furniture. Well, I've decided I'd like to keep things under control."

"We surely wish you two the best. Both of you have had enough rough times. But we'll miss havin' you here at the hotel. I don't know what attracts more guests—your pies or that sparkle in your smile!"

"My smile isn't sparkling tonight," Pepper commented. "I'm going straight to bed. I'll see you in the morning!"

"Good night, Pepper, honey."

"Good night, Mrs. Mac."

The parlor was just as hot as the kitchen, but flooded with tobacco smoke and loud voices. Bob McCurley was in the center of a crowd of men, waving his hands and talking about "the biggest bull elk in the state of Colorado."

She scurried past the men to the foot of the stairs.

"Miss Pepper!" a young man's voice called out.

She turned to see a man in a tight-collared shirt wave at her. "Miss Pepper, I wonder if you'd like to join us for conversation? We'd surely enjoy your company."

"Not tonight, Little Bob. I'm very tired."

"I'll be leaving on the stage tomorrow."

"Have a nice trip."

The tall, strong-shouldered twenty-three-year-old with a wispy blond beard walked toward her as she stood on the first level of stairs. "Are you actually getting married?"

"Yes. Two weeks from today."

"I don't suppose there's anything I could do or say to make you change your mind?"

"Little Bob, why on earth would you want to do that?"

"You know, Miss Pepper, you're the loveliest woman I've ever seen in my life!" he gushed.

She thought about how messy, sweaty, sticky, and sore she felt.

"Well, you've just got to get out and meet more women, Little Bob. Now good night." She took several steps up the wide staircase.

"You know, Miss Pepper, I don't really have to go tomorrow. If you want me to stay, just say the word."

She glared at him. *You've got to be kidding! For what possible reason would I want you to stay? Go! Go! Go!*

He leaned on one foot and then the other. "Of course, I need to get to . . . you know . . . Denver and . . . ," he stammered.

"Goodbye, Little Bob." She nodded and scurried up the stairs.

"Miss Pepper!" he called out.

She stopped at the top of the stairs and spun around. Putting her hands on her hips and sighing, she glanced down at the wide, blue eyes of Robert T. Gundersen, Jr.

"Eh, Miss Pepper . . . what can I bring you from Denver?"

"What?"

"I—I wanted to bring you a present. What would you like?"

"A wedding present is always appreciated. Tap and I would appreciate having a few new things for the home."

"Actually, I was thinkin' of somethin' more, you know, personal."

"Little Bob, maybe you ought to step out there and get some cool air. Now good night."

"Good night, Miss Pepper. I'll be thinkin' of you all the time I'm in Denver."

She shrugged and turned toward her room, leaving him gazing up the stairs at the back of her dress as she disappeared from his sight.

Pepper was dismayed to find her room as warm as the kitchen. She plopped down in the chair next to the bed and pulled off her shoes and stockings. Even the hard, polished wood floor felt warm to her toes as she hung her dress and brushed it down.

Pepper washed up in the tepid water from the basin and then stared for a moment at her flannel nightgown before pulling it over her head.

I'd rather not wear it, but I suppose I'll be freezing by morning. At least it's not sweaty . . . yet.

After combing through her wavy, blonde hair for several minutes, she pulled back the hunter green comforter on the bed and fluffed up the large down pillows. Retrieving a piece of paper and pencil from the top of the dresser, Pepper sprawled across the bed.

She began a new list on the paper under the heading, "Things to discuss with T. A." Somewhere between points 15 and 20, Pepper laid her head on the pillow and fell asleep.

The long, ruffled off-white gown billowed from her shoulders to the floor. The high lace collar and sleeve insets provided a teasing contrast. Dangling diamond earrings seemed to catch the sparkle in her eyes.

Pepper stood at the full-length mirror gazing at the bride.

Your nose is too wide, and your chin too narrow. But I can tell you one thing, you'll turn his head tonight, Pepper Paige!

She stepped out into a large ballroom with a high ceiling and two magnificent chandeliers. The room was buzzing with men in dress frock coats and women in gorgeous gowns.

At the far end of the room a twelve-piece orchestra began to play a waltz. A strong, rugged-looking man wearing a ruffled shirt strolled toward her.

"Mr. Andrews said that it was my turn to dance with the bride!" he announced.

"Oh . . . yes . . . well, certainly. Eh, where is Tap?"

"I think he stepped outside."

They twirled around the perimeter of the room, weaving in and out of other laughing, talking dancers. Finally they spun to a stop, and the man bowed and departed.

Pepper was tired. She could feel perspiration on her neck. Her feet were warm and tight in the shoes. She was thinking about stepping outside to find Tap when an older, slightly graying man touched her arm.

"There you are, my dear! Well, well . . . you promised to dance with me, remember?"

"Governor!"

"My, that Andrews is a lucky fellow."

They swung out on the floor. "Thank you, sir." She tried to smile. *Now where did that Tap scoot off to?*

Pepper scanned the room as they spun through the crowd.

This time when the music stopped, her feet ached. Her hair surged down over her right ear. She carefully tried to wipe the beads of sweat off her forehead with a white linen hankie that had been tucked into her sleeve.

Tap Andrews, I want to dance with you!

But it was a dark-complected man with a neatly trimmed goatee that approached her next. After him came a short, round, bald man with laughing eyes and sweaty palms. Then there was the army captain . . . and the cowboy with big Spanish rowels on his spurs . . . and the Chinese cook still wearing his dirty white apron and hat.

Finally Pepper pulled herself away. She was so tired she just wanted to collapse. Limping in the pinching shoes toward the big double doors of the ballroom, she tried to tuck her wavy hair back into the combs on the back of her head.

Expecting to feel a cool winter breeze when she stepped outside, she was shocked when a blast of hot desert air hit her and she spotted a man wearing a clerical collar staring across the sage and cactus.

This isn't Colorado!

"Reverend? Reverend Houston, have you seen Tap?"

The smiling clergyman turned to her. "No, my child, Mr. Andrews has not appeared. I'll let you know as soon as he arrives, and then we can get the service started."

"Started? You mean we haven't said the vows yet?"

"My heavens, no!"

"But—but . . . that's not right! That's not the way I have it organized! We don't dance until after the service!"

"Well, well, my dear, things don't always go as planned, do
they?"

She shoved her hands to her hips. "They do in my wedding,
Parson. They do in my wedding!"

The morning light of another cold Colorado day was peeking
around the base of the curtains in her room when Pepper awoke,
buried deep under the quilts and comforters on her bed at the
McCurley Hotel. She rolled to her back and kicked all the covers
to the floor.

*Lord, why do I keep having that dream? Everything WILL go
as planned! Won't it?*

A voice at the door brought her to her feet. She clutched her
robe. "Pepper dear? I'm afraid we won't be able to go out to the
ranch today."

She opened the door slightly and peeked out at Mrs. McCurley.
"Why? What's wrong?"

"We had more guests come in last night. Mr. McCurley says we
just shouldn't take off, being full up and all. Oh, but you take the
day off."

"Really?"

"Honey, I'm sure you could find your way out to the ranch on
your own."

"But it might not look proper."

"Pepper, in this weather there ain't no one lookin'." Mrs.
McCurley grinned. "Besides I know you two need to make plans.
Tap can drive you back tonight."

"Well . . . I think I just might." She shut the door and then suddenly jerked it open again. "Mrs. Mac, does Mr. McCurley have
time to harness the buggy for me?"

"I'll see that someone gets it ready. I think some fresh air will
do you good."

"I believe you're right. Say, is it hot in the hotel, or is it just me?"

"Oh, it's Mr. McCurley burning that white pine. You know how it blazes. The new guests were almost frozen when they arrived—from Arizona, I believe. I guess he's tryin' to make it feel like home. Oh! I'll be! I came up here to tell you there's a man downstairs eatin' breakfast that I think you should talk to before you leave."

"You don't mean Little Bob, do you?"

"Oh, my, no. He's a persistent young man, isn't he? No, this fellow came in from Arizona last night. Says his name is Abel Cedar."

"Who?"

"Abel Cedar. Claims to be headed out to the ranch to visit with his old friend Zachariah Hatcher."

"Cedar? He's—he's Suzanne Cedar's brother!"

"That's sort of the way I figure."

"What did you tell him?"

"Nothin'. But that's why I figured you would want to talk with him a spell and save him a trip."

"Yes. I'll . . . I'll . . . be down shortly and talk with him."

Closing the door, Pepper stood in front of the dresser and stared into the mirror.

Lord, I promised if someone . . . ever came looking for Suzanne, I'd give them her belongings . . . and her money. We were going to use those funds to get the ranch started. I've been workin' here at the hotel so we could save that money for something more important. And the dresses—the pretty dresses. I can't give it all up. I just can't!

Pepper dragged the big trunk from the corner of her room and opened it up.

The jewelry, the handbags—what am I going to tell Tap? Why isn't he here? He'd know what to do!

I knew it would happen.

I always knew I wouldn't get to keep any of it.

Thirty minutes later Pepper scooted down the stairs wearing her long green dress and heavy coat, the only items left in her wardrobe that she had brought out of the dance hall. She grasped Suzanne Cedar's Bible.

Mrs. McCurley stood near the front door talking to a very tall, thin man with long hair and unkempt beard.

"Pepper, this is Mr. Abel Cedar."

He tipped his worn derby hat and smiled, revealing two gold teeth.

"Pleased to meet you, ma'am. Mrs. McCurley said you wanted to talk to me."

"Eh, yes, I do. Can we sit in the parlor, Mrs. Mac?"

"Certainly, dear."

Pepper led the way into the wood-paneled parlor and slid onto a padded oak deacon's bench.

"Mr. Cedar, I understand you are on your way to see Mr. Zachariah Hatcher."

"Yes. Of course, I haven't seen Hatch for several years, but I understand he was finally able to buy that little ranch up on the border. Do you know him?"

"Well . . . no. But, well . . . Mr. Cedar . . . I don't know a kind way to say this. But Mr. Hatcher was killed down in Arizona last fall. There was some sort of Indian skirmish south of Mexican Wells—"

"You don't say! Hatcher killed? I can't . . . I've traveled all this way. . . . You don't say!" he stammered. "Doesn't that sink your ship!"

"Eh . . . I have a little more to tell you."

"I hope it's better news than that."

Lord, help me now! "Well, I think . . . it is going to be worse."

"Oh, no!"

Pepper took a big breath. *I am not going to cry!*

"Mr. Cedar, did you come from Kentucky and have a sister named Suzanne?"

"How did you know that?"

"Eh . . . Mr. Cedar, I'm havin' a real hard time telling you this. It's that . . . well, your father and your . . ." Pepper could feel tears slip out of the corners of her eyes and slide to the edge of her nose.

"Oh, listen." He sighed. "I don't blame you for worrying. But I know all about it."

"You do?"

"Yeah, I ran across a fellow from my home town. He told me Father died, Mother sold the place, and she and Suzanne moved to Chicago."

"Well, that's not all. Your—"

"Yes, I heard that Mama, bless her soul, died in Chicago."

"And . . ."

"And what?" he asked.

"Your sister."

"What about my sister? She moved out to California and married some big rancher. I figure to go look her up after I work my claim."

"Your claim?"

"Yep, I found color just north of Bisbee down in Arizona territory. I was hoping that Zachariah Hatcher would stake me so I could get it developed proper and—"

"Mr. Cedar, please excuse my interrupting, but my heart's about to burst. Mr. Cedar . . . your sister Suzanne is dead."

"Say that again."

"Suzanne was on her way to Colorado, not California, to marry none other than Zachariah Hatcher when she was in a stage wreck. She was badly injured and died in my room—that is, at the place where I worked. At Pingree Hill between here and Ft. Collins."

"I don't believe it! Not Suzanne, too!"

"I know it's a shock. Here's her Bible. I have dearly enjoyed reading it over the past few months."

"Suzanne's Bible? Where did you get this?" he demanded.

"I told you, she died in my—room."

The tall man slumped his shoulders and stared at the floor. "It's like . . . like my whole life, all my—dreams . . . and family—everything just blown away in a bad wind storm."

"I have her trunk in my room. I've been keeping things, not knowing what to do with them. I can have them packed very quickly."

"What kind of things?" he asked.

"Clothes, shoes—things like that. Mr. Cedar, we gave her the best burial we could at Pingree Hill. The Reverend Houston stopped by and said prayers over her. She was a fine Christian lady."

"Yeah. That's Suzanne."

"I want to confess, Mr. Cedar, I, eh, I've worn some of her things. They were so beautiful, and I didn't know what to do with them."

"You sort of remind me of Suzanne—the yellow hair, the smile, even your manner. When you first came into the room with Mrs. McCurley, I thought of my sister."

"Why, thank you, Mr. Cedar. I take that as a great compliment. Would you like to come up and get the trunk?"

"I really don't have . . . It will be . . . ," he stammered.

"The money! I almost forgot the money!" Pepper brushed back a tear and took the Bible from his hand. Then pulling out a fat envelope from the front, she handed it to Abel Cedar.

"What's this?"

"She had this money. I was saving it for—"

"How much is in here?" he shouted.

"Eh, $1,600. But I spent about $100. I promise I'll save it up and pay you back."

"This is my stake! This is it. Jehovah jireh!"

"I beg your pardon?"

"The Lord provides! This is what I need to develop the claim. And it came from Suzy girl! I can't believe this! This is . . . it's the worst and best day of my life all in one."

"I'm glad it's not all bad news. Would you like to go up and get the trunk now?"

"A bunch of clothes?"

"Yes, and some small pieces of jewelry and—"

"Miss Paige, I can't believe you held this for me. I don't know many people with your honesty and integrity. You didn't even know I was coming!"

"Well, to tell you the truth I—"

"And you took care of Suzanne at the end of her life? Well, Lord bless you, Miss Paige. The Lord bless you!"

"Really, I didn't have any say in the—"

Abel Cedar jumped to his feet. "I am on my way to Arizona to develop that gold mine!"

"And the trunk?"

"For your benevolence in dealing with my Suzy, I want you to have her things."

"Are you joking?"

"No. I implore you to keep it. I couldn't take any of it with me anyway."

"And the Bible?"

"You keep it. I have one of my own."

"I couldn't. I . . ."

He leaned over and grabbed her by the shoulders. "You deserve it, and I must be off. If I don't get that taken care of quickly, I'll lose my claim."

He scurried toward the wooden coat rack.

"But don't you want to see the grave site?"

"I'll come back as soon as I get that gold in Arizona. Then I can put up an iron fence and a big marble marker."

He tipped his hat and scooted toward the front door.

"How about that $100? Where shall I send it?"

"It is your pay for being such a fine executor of Suzanne's estate. Good day, Miss Paige!"

He was out the door before she was able to mumble, "Good day, Mr. Cedar."

She walked back up the stairs slowly and reentered her room. Changing into a stylish, lace-trimmed dress, she looked over each piece of the wardrobe.

It's mine now, isn't it, Lord? It's not pretend anymore— always knowing it belongs to someone else. It's really mine! You heard him!"

She strolled down the stairs with gloves, ear muffs, and a hooded cape that had once belonged to Miss Suzanne Cedar.

Mrs. McCurley was waiting for her. "Mr. Cedar lit out of here in a hurry."

"Everything's okay—I think. Very well, considering all. Now I really have something to talk to Tap about! Do you know if the carriage is ready?"

"I put a few supplies in the buggy for you, including one of your peach pies."

"But don't you need it here with all the crowd?"

"That cowboy of yours needs a little spoilin'. I'll make us a big batch of pooch, and everyone will be happy for one night anyway."

"Pooch?"

"Canned tomatoes, white sugar, and bread."

"They eat that?"

"Land-a-Goshen, yes. But I don't have to tell them my recipe. Now go on. It's a clear day. You go have fun, but you be a good girl, you hear me?"

"Yes, Mother."

The round-faced woman with short, gray hair smiled from ear to ear. "Well, a girl fixin' for a weddin' needs a mama, that's for sure. But I don't mean to cause you no offense."

"Mrs. Mac, you can mother me anytime you want. My mama died when I was fourteen. It was a very long time ago."

The blast of cold air hit Pepper as she stepped out onto the hotel porch. She took a big, deep breath and stretched her arms. Her head was still swimming.

The hot coals that Bob McCurley had placed in the metal fire box below the floorboard of the buggy felt warm for about the first ten minutes of the ride. After that they were just plain hot.

Pepper finally pulled the lap quilt off her legs and shoved it down on the lid of the box to relieve the heat on her shoes. The brisk December air burned a refreshing coldness against her face. She loosened the hood of her cape to allow some of the breeze to wash back across her ears and neck.

It will be pretty cold after dark. Tap will be driving the rig, and I'll be sitting next to him and, well, it won't be all that cold!

You know, Lord, I'm not sure at all what You're feeling about me and Tap getting married. But I want it bad, Lord. Real bad. It's like You giving me a chance to do something with my life that I don't have to be ashamed of.

But I've got to tell him we can't count on Suzanne's money any-more. It's all right. We can get by.

After resting the horse once when she crossed the frozen creek bed, Pepper rolled on up into the hills toward the ranch, nibbling on one of the corn fritters Mrs. Mac had stashed in a basket with the pie.

The fire in the box had died by the time the ranch house came into view. It was the only dwelling between McCurleys' and the Wyoming line, and Pepper was always excited when she spied it.

There's smoke coming from the chimney! Tap's home. He'll see me driving in and come bursting out the front door any minute.

The sprawling, unpainted ranch house with covered porch running the length of the building looked bleak perched on a blanket of snow and surrounded by a scattering of leafless cottonwoods. The towering barn, wreathed by weathered corrals, occupied the east side of the vast yard.

She watched the door right up until she stopped the rig by the ice-covered brass hitching post in the middle of the yard.

Tap's probably in the kitchen. I wonder if I should tell him about Abel Cedar right away—or wait until we visit for a while? Maybe I'll just sneak in and surprise him!

Climbing out of the buggy, she retrieved the basket with the pie in one hand and her handbag in the other. The snow crunched beneath her feet as she tried to step lightly toward the porch.

If he's standing there peeking out of the window at me sneaking up like this, I'm going to feel like a fool!

The glass panes on both windows seemed frosted over, and she couldn't see inside the house at all. The front porch creaked in the popping manner of frozen wood.

This is ridiculous! There's no way to sneak up on a man like Tap.

Pepper propped her handbag on top of the basket and slid her gloved right hand across the black iron door handle. The heavy wooden door slid open without any sound, and she stepped into the musty-smelling front room. She quietly closed the door behind her and waited for her eyes to adjust to the darkness.

I don't hear anything. Maybe he's out in the barn.

Placing the basket and handbag on the table littered with hand tools and strips of leather, she glanced over at the grand piano in the center of the huge rectangular room.

A saddle? Now he's using the piano as a saddle repair bench? He's obviously not expecting me. This room's a—a horrid mess!

Pepper tiptoed toward the kitchen.

It's awfully warm in here.

Reaching the kitchen doorway, she stood for a moment and stared at its contents.

He hasn't washed a single dish since I was here last time! Does he think I come out here just to clean his house? 'Course, he didn't know I was coming. But at least after the wedding, it will be my mess, too.

Pepper pulled off her hooded cape and draped it on an empty peg by the pantry door. Then she tugged off her heavy coat.

He can just put away the buggy himself. The first thing I should do is heat some water for washing these dishes. How come I always forget to bring an apron? No, the first thing I'll do is break apart that fire. It's way too warm in here.

She was halfway across the front room when the rocking chair facing the fireplace caught her eye.

Tap?

He sat there wrapped in a wool blanket, chin on his chest in deep sleep.

He must have been up all night. Probably something with the cows. Poor man. He looks worn out, covered head to toe with a blanket. He must have gotten frozen out there!

Well, I know what can warm him up!

She slipped up behind the chair.

He's definitely got to get his hair cut before the wedding.

She put her hands over his eyes and whispered, "Hey, cowboy, how would you like those dreams to come true?"

"What?" A strange voice choked as the man in the chair leaped straight up, clutching for his holstered revolver. The gray and white cat by the hearth flew wildly toward the kitchen.

Pepper jumped back and shouted, "Who are you?"

3

"Did I die and go to heaven?" the man wearing a black vest and a blanket across his shoulders mumbled through half-open eyes.

"Who *are* you?" Pepper demanded again. "What are you doing here? Where's Tap? What do you mean leading me on to think that you were him?" She could feel her face flush with anger as she tried to remember where Tap kept his shotgun.

"Whoa, lady. I'm sorry. Look, I, eh . . ."

"Get out of here!" she screamed. "Get out of here right now!"

"Look, ma'am, I'm sorry. I was just sleepin'. Been ridin' all night. Tap told me to—I didn't . . . say, you're that yellow-haired gal from McCurleys', ain't ya?"

"So what?" she yelled.

"Well, you sure got that old Tap hooked. All he talks about is the weddin'."

She could feel the tension begin to leave her throat. "Really? He talks about it? Who are you?"

"I'm Wiley. I work at the Rafter R. Well, I used to work at the Rafter R up in Wyomin'. I'm a friend of Tap's, but I'll be goin'. I didn't know you was comin' and—"

"Wait." Pepper sighed and stepped back toward the piano. "Listen, I guess I kind of . . . well, I assumed you were Tap."

"Yes, ma'am, I sort of got the idee that you weren't exactly gleeful to see me."

"Where is he?"

"He rode out lookin' for the trail of some rustlers."

"Someone stole our cattle—eh, his cattle?"

"No. They stole Rafter R cows and pushed them down this way. I rode in last night to warn him that Fightin' Ed and crew would be comin' down here lookin' for Rafter R beef, and there could be trouble."

"What kind of trouble?"

"Fightin' Ed Casey is on the prowl, and he thinks Tap's rustled those Herefords."

"So Tap went to see if he could find the dangerous rustlers all by himself?"

"Well, eh, actually I think he was just scoutin' for sign. He ought to be back soon. I was catchin' up on a little sleep. I surely didn't aim to alarm you none, ma'am."

"Look, eh, I didn't mean to, you know, chase you off. Tap's friends are my friends. Why don't you just stay there by the fire and warm up. I'm going to see if I can clean up that kitchen before it petrifies."

"Thanks, Miss, eh—"

"Everyone calls me Pepper."

"And I can certainly see why. Miss Pepper, I'm feeling rested, so I reckon I'll ride out and see what Tap found. I'll tell him you're here. I don't think he was expectin' you until next week."

"That's obvious!" She waved her hand around at the junk piled about the room.

Wiley slapped on his hat. His spurs jingled as he stepped outside. Pausing on the porch, he stuck his head back in the room.

"Miss Pepper, I'll put your rig away. Say, Tap said you don't have any sisters—is that right?"

"I'm an only child and . . . Why did you ask me that?"

A wide smile broke across Wiley's face. She was surprised to see straight, white teeth. "I was just thinkin' about . . ."

"Oh. Yes . . . well . . ." She blushed. "Thank you for that compliment, Mr. Wiley."

"Just Wiley, no mister. I'll go find Tap."

"Tell him there's a peach pie waiting for him."

"Frankly, ma'am," Wiley pushed his hat to the back of his head, "I don't reckon he'll need any extra encouragement."

"You'll stay for supper, I hope?"

"Actually I'm stayin' out in the tack room a few days."

You are? Not after December 22 you aren't!

Pepper stared at the frosty window as Wiley drove the horse and buggy through the giant double doors of the barn.

I will never, never sneak up on any man ever again! What a fool! I could have been shot—or worse!

After building a fire in the cookstove in the kitchen under two big pots of very cold water, she began cleaning up the front room. She trimmed the lamps and lit each one. Then she stacked the saddle, tools, and pieces of leather in a corner behind the table. After putting away boots, shirts, dishes, brass casings, and assorted pieces of spurs, bridles, and guns, Pepper found a halfway clean dusting rag.

When she finished sweeping the room, she slipped out on the front porch to enjoy the freezing breeze brush across her face and hands.

The kitchen proved to be a more formidable task. By the time the dishes were clean, the floor mopped, and the food put back into the pantry, sweat rolled down her face and dripped on her dress.

"Well, Sal," she addressed the wide-eyed cat, "I'm surely glad I didn't have to stay and work at McCurleys'. Just a nice restful day at the ranch. I ought to get supper started beings there's going to be company . . . but I'm tired!"

Pepper strolled back into the front room and plopped down at the piano bench.

I wonder if I'll get lonesome out here? I mean, after a while? At the hotel people are always coming and going. At April's, I dreamed about a nice, quiet, isolated house like this!

She lifted the cover off the keys and began to peck with one finger. Each note sounded muffled and dull.

"All right, Andrews, what did you do to my piano?"

She propped up the top of the grand piano and found a shirt and a leather vest crammed against the strings.

A dirty clothes hamper? You're using a grand piano for a clothes hamper?

She carried the items into the bedroom and flung them against the wall on top of a stack of what looked like dirty clothes, towels, and bedding.

"I'm not cleaning your bedroom, Mr. Tapadera Andrews! At least not for another thirteen days!"

She was startled to hear a sharp rap at the door. Tucking her hair up in the combs, she scooted across the front room.

Why is Tap knocking at the door?

She took a deep breath, prepared a smile, and flung open the door so hard it banged against the wall. The short man in the heavy topcoat jumped back.

"Excuse me, ma'am," he stammered, pulling off his hat and exposing a nearly bald head.

"Who are you?"

"I'm Mr. H. F. Rawlins, the new manager of the First Mercantile Bank of Fort Collins."

"A banker?"

"Yes, ma'am."

"Are you lost?"

"Eh, I hope not, but I am awfully cold. Would it be proper for me to step in by your fire while we chat?"

"Oh, yes, certainly. Come in."

He ambled toward the fireplace. The redness in his cheeks signaled a long buggy ride. The cat met him halfway and began to meow and rub against his boots.

"I'm afraid I've let the fire dwindle. Go ahead and build it up if you'd like. Can I get you a cup of coffee?"

"Mrs. Hatcher, that would be the nicest thing that has happened to me all week."

"Oh, I'm not Mrs. Hatcher."

Squatting next to the fire, the man placed several more sticks of wood on the coals. "Oh, my, don't tell me I've come to the wrong ranch." He pulled some papers out of his overcoat pocket.

"I'm looking for a Mr. Zachariah Hatcher's ranch."

"Well, this is Hatcher's ranch. . . . I mean, it used to be his ranch."

"Used to be?"

"Yes, Mr. Hatcher is deceased, and the place belongs to a Mr. Tapadera Andrews now. Perhaps you should wait and have Mr. Andrews explain."

"Oh, that is puzzling news! Why, I had no idea!"

"You knew Mr. Hatcher?"

"Actually no. The former manager made the loan, and now he's moved off to Sacramento. I've just taken over, and I'm trying to clear up all the accounts."

"Loan? Accounts? What do you mean?"

"Well, I'm sure your husband knew when he bought the place from—"

"The truth is, Mr. Andrews is not my husband—yet. We're getting married in a couple weeks."

"How nice."

"And I—I live down at McCurleys'. I just came out for the day."

"Oh, splendid! You know how to get to McCurleys'! I wanted to stay there tonight, and for the life of me I couldn't figure out how to get there from here. Maybe you could draw me a map or something."

"Certainly, but what was this about a loan?"

"Well, Mr. Hatcher still owes over two thousand dollars on the loan he secured when he bought this ranch. The payment was due December 1, but as I said, things at the bank have been a little disorganized."

"Two thousand dollars?"

"Actually $2,089.45."

"And you came out to collect?"

"Well, that would be glorious! But there is a thirty-day grace period. I won't have to foreclose until December 31."

"I—I don't know if Mr. Andrews was aware that he was assuming a loan."

"Oh, yes. It's right there on the patent deed. If you'll bring me your copy of the deed, I'll show you the provision."

"Eh, I think maybe you should wait for Mr. Andrews to return. Can I . . . eh, get you a piece of peach pie with your coffee?"

"Most assuredly! Splendid, Miss, eh, Miss—"

"Paige. Miss Pepper Paige."

"Thank you for your hospitality, Miss Paige. You'd be surprised how nasty some people treat us bankers. Why, sometimes they won't even give me the time of day. The last couple I spoke with threatened to throw me out on my ear!"

Actually, Mr. Banker, I was considering shooting you myself.

Tap watched seven Rafter R drovers ride up from all sides.

"Sorry, the fire's about dead, boys. If you scruff up a little dry wood, we can all warm up." Looking up at a cowboy with a long, black handlebar mustache, he nodded. "Howdy, Quail. How's the winter treatin' you?"

The cowboy tipped his hat. "Tap, 'fraid this ain't a social occasion. There's Rafter R bovines running with your TC longhorns."

Casey pulled Andrews's revolver from its holster and tossed it into the snow.

"How many tracks did you follow down here?"

"Looked like four men."

"You ride down there about a hundred yards to the south, and you'll find four tracks leadin' out of here. Those are your rustlers," Tap instructed.

"I'll check it out!" Quail spurred his mount and rode away to the south.

"Don't matter," Fighting Ed hollered. "They might have done the dirty work, but you was the ring leader."

"Why would I raid the Rafter R and then just push them over the state line? Those four were fixin' to steal my cows, too."

"Why didn't you shoot 'em?" one of the cowboys called out.

"They hadn't committed any crime in Colorado—yet. But they weren't all exactly in good health when they left. I was plannin' on cuttin' out the Rafter R Herefords as soon as my feet warmed up and drivin' 'em back up to the border."

"Oh, they'll git back to the Rafter R range, all right. But no thanks to you." Fighting Ed's tall-crowned hat made his head look long and narrow.

"Tap's right about four ridin' south," Quail reported as he rode back to the others. "At least one was drippin' blood."

"There's a little red around this campfire, too." Another of the men pointed to the snow at Andrews's feet. "Some of 'em are carrying lead. Maybe we ought to try to catch them."

"That bunch is runnin' like wounded wolves. But it's too close to Christmas to get yourselves killed. Why don't you just round up those white faces and take them home. Graze them separate, and if they're still lookin' healthy by July, turn 'em out with the others. That Spanish fever will show by then."

"I'll give the orders around here," Casey snarled.

"While you're decidin' what the orders are, I'm pullin' on my boots before my feet freeze solid."

Fighting Ed waved the revolver at Tap's head. "Stay standin'! You ain't doin' nothin', Andrews!"

Tap glanced up at the mounted Rafter R hands. "You ever see an unarmed man get shot in the back for just puttin' on his boots?"

Several shook their heads.

Tap sat down on his saddle, brushed the snow off his socks, and began pulling the cold, stiff boots onto his aching feet. Standing up, he grabbed the tabs on his left boot and yanked it on. Then he did the same with the right. His eyes briefly glanced at the Winchester propped against the granite rock.

I could get one shot off before taking a few. If I dropped Fightin' Ed, the others might not be so anxious. But, Lord, there's got to be something I can do besides shoot everybody who rides onto the ranch!

"Well, what's the order, Fightin' Ed? You goin' to go get your cows, or you goin' to shoot me in the back? You askin' these men to take part in the murder of an unarmed Colorado rancher?"

"Hangin' a cattle rustler ain't murder!"

"You men think that's the way a Colorado jury would see it? Folks down here aren't too impressed by those big Wyomin' ranches."

"If we string you up, there wouldn't be a need to have a jury, would there?" Fighting Ed growled.

"You goin' to hang Wiley, too? He knows I didn't rustle any cows. He's sittin' down there warmin' his toes by my fireplace."

"I hired on to punch cows, not kill unarmed men," Quail piped up. "We'd better gather those cows and get them movin' north before we run smack dab into the night."

Fighting Ed's breath fogged out in front of him. Pointing at a gaunt man, he muttered, "You stay here and keep a bead on him. We'll take him with us back to the Rafter R and then see what a Wyomin' jury will decide."

"Now that's a mighty fine idea, boss," the cowboy replied. "And what should I do if he tries to escape?"

"Shoot him."

"I was hopin' you'd say that!"

Within a few moments, Tap had his hands tied behind his back and was seated on his saddle. Casey and the others rode down the hill to cut out the Herefords. The lone cowboy wearing worn black gauntlets circled the fire, trying to stir up the coals while holding his revolver in one hand.

"Andrews, ain't this somethin'? Just you and me again."

Tap stared into the man's narrow eyes. "Do I know you?" he asked.

"Drew Blackstone."

Wiley said Blackstone was the only Rafter R man that might shoot him!

"I don't recognize the name."

"Oh, you know me, all right. Two years ago in that little Cantina in the Mule Mountains in Arizona—a ruckus about a soiled dove stealin' my two hundred dollars."

"Were you that blubberin' drunk who tried to bushwhack the pretty Mexican dance-hall girl?"

"She poached my money, and you know it, Andrews!"

"You got what you paid for."

"I didn't git two hundred dollars' worth."

"It might have been a bad business deal or bad luck, but the money belonged to her."

Blackstone rubbed his eyes with the back of his gloves. "Now I'll tell you what's bad luck for you. That's havin' me be the one to guard you. You see, I jist know that you're goin' to try and escape."

"That would be rather foolish of me, wouldn't it? Especially since I'm tied up."

"Desperate men do foolish things."

Tap thought he saw movement in the piñon pines behind the man. He stared back at the coals.

The gun-toting Drew Blackstone continued to circle the fire. "'Course, I cain't figure how you ever got out of A.T.P. Ol' man Perez told me you got hung down in Yuma."

"He lied."

Someone's watchin' us! Can't be Fightin' Ed and crew . . . can it? "Nobody gets hung at Yuma. The heat gets them first."

"You sure you don't feel like tryin' to escape?" Blackstone baited him.

"Nope. But I would appreciate it if you built up the fire and let me stand and turn around so I could warm up my hands. Maybe you could start cookin' supper. Me and the boys will be mighty hungry. How did you land this fire-tendin' job, Blackstone? Is this all they had left for drunks who can't ride, rope, or wrangle?"

"Why you . . ."

Tap ducked to avoid the swinging barrel of the revolver. His hat slowed down the blow that struck above his left ear and cracked into his shoulder blade. He toppled off the saddle into the snow away from the fire and tried to roll to his back and fend off another blow with his feet.

But it was Blackstone who slumped unconscious next to him in the snow. Wiley stood over him, smiling and holding his '73 carbine.

"He rammed his head into the barrel. But don't worry, the barrel's still all right."

"Wiley! I was hopin' that was you hidin' in the piñons."

"You expectin' someone else? Maybe that yellow-haired girl?"

"Not hardly."

"That's too bad 'cause she's down there at the house waitin' for you."

"She's what?"

"Look, Andrews, are you just goin' to lay there in the snow bleedin', or are you goin' to invite me to sit down at your fire?"

"You might untie me."

"Well, I'll be! Are you tied up?" He pulled a knife from his belt and cut the narrow leather laces that had bound Tap's hands behind him.

Andrews rolled to his feet, brushed off the snow, and rubbed his aching head and shoulder.

"What's this about Pepper?"

"She showed up about two hours ago."

"By herself?"

"Yeah."

"Are you sure it was Pepper?"

"Purdy yellow hair, green eyes, and a dimpled smile that would make a dead dog wag its tail. A fancy dress that was cut—"

"Okay, okay. What's she doin' there?"

"Well, she was unduly daunted when I wasn't you. But what I want to know is how did you let Blackstone get the jump on you?"

"I was tryin' to warm my feet."

"What?"

"Never mind. Did you see Fightin' Ed and the others?"

"Yeah, but I was following your trail, ridin' the high line. I don't think they spotted me."

"I thought you said they wouldn't be down here until tomorrow."

"I was wrong. It looked to me like the Rafter R boys were about done gatherin'. You ready to light shuck and head for the ranch?"

"Nope. Old Fightin' Ed would just come after us, right?"

"Yeah. I reckon he's decided you're a genuine cattle rustler. You don't aim to shoot it out, do you?"

"I hope not. Help me prop up this great gunman."

Tap and Wiley sat the unconscious Blackstone in the snow and leaned him against the granite boulder. After tying his hands to his feet, they gagged him with his own bandanna and replaced his hat.

"You rapped him pretty good with the rifle barrel."

"I was in a hurry. You looked like you were in trouble."

"Me? I had him right where I wanted him."

"He was about to shoot you!"

"About to be shot is not the same as actually being shot," Tap teased. "Besides, you don't mean to tell me that Drew here would shoot a man who has his hands tied behind his back?"

"What do we do now?" Wiley asked.

"You ride on back up into the piñons and wait. If things go right, I'll ride up to you in a few minutes."

"And if they go wrong?"

"Well . . . well, I guess you'll have to go back and marry that gal with the yellow hair yourself."

"Don't tempt me, Andrews!"

"Nothin's goin' to go wrong. Go on, get out of sight!"

By the time Casey and three of his crew returned, Tap had saddled Brownie and built up the fire. He was sitting on the boulder next to Blackstone with his hands behind his back. His right hand clutched the Colt .44.

"Drew," Casey shouted, "come on, wake up! Let's—what the . . ."

Tap swung the pistol around and had Fighting Ed covered before he could even reach for his gun. "I'm glad you're done with the roundup. Sorry you can't stay and warm up, but I know you're in a hurry to be gettin' back to Wyoming."

"What's goin' on here?" Casey demanded.

"Well, Drew here got me mad. So I just made him take a little nap."

The bound man was trying to mumble something.

"Quail, how about you helpin' this *hombre malo* to his pony?"

"What do you think you're doin'?" Casey shouted.

"Look, you got your cows. The four rustlers are deep in the mountains by now, and you've got Blackstone with nothin' more than a bad headache. Why not go back to the bunkhouse and warm up?"

"Sounds good to me," Quail mumbled as he untied Blackstone and helped him to his feet.

"Those four came back and ambushed me!" Drew snarled.

"If they did, then they're sittin' in those trees with guns on you right now. If I rustled those cows, I surely would have shot a worthless character like Blackstone, wouldn't I?"

"Andrews . . . if one more head of Rafter R stock is found down here on the Triple Creek, I'll shoot you on sight," Fighting Ed puffed.

"Quail, get him off my ranch! The rest of you boys, if Fightin' Ed steers you down here again, have him ride way out in the lead by himself. I don't want a bullet to go strayin' off and hit one of you. Now get out of here before I really get mad!"

"I'm not done with you, Andrews!" Casey shouted. "I'm not done until I run you clean out of this country!"

"You want to have it out, Casey?" Tap hollered. "Get down off that horse. Boys, back up and give us room. Come on, Casey, you and me, just the two of us. Let's get it over with."

The others around Fighting Ed, including Drew Blackstone, rode their horses away from their boss.

"I'm not puttin' up with this anymore. Get down here and make good on your word," Andrews demanded.

"I'm—I'm not goin' up against an Arizona gunslinger who's already got his gun drawn!" Casey protested.

Andrews jammed his Colt back into the holster. "Go ahead. Go for it. Or get off my ranch!"

Fighting Ed turned his horse and spurred back toward the others holding the cows in the draw west of the campfire.

Quail turned back to Tap. "We won't make it off your place by nightfall."

"About seven miles north of here is a little grove of red fir trees. There's still meadow grass on the east side peeking above the snow. Leave the cattle there and make camp in that circle of firs. There's a stack of firewood under the biggest tree. I got stuck up there one time and nearly froze, so I stashed some wood. Help yourself."

"Thanks, Tap." Quail nodded. "Is Wiley back in the piñons?"

"Yeah."

"That's what I figured. I just might be ridin' down your way one of these days, too." Quail trotted off after the others.

The Rafter R crew had barely started north when Tap kicked out the fire and rode into the piñon pine trees to join up with Wiley. The two rode south in silence for several minutes. Tap and Brownie led the way. The sun hung low in the west, and he could feel the temperature drop. His cheeks were already numb, but he refused to cover them with his bandanna.

"Tap," Wiley called out, "I heard you baitin' Fightin' Ed. What would you have done if he took you up on it?"

"What?"

"What if Casey would have jumped off his horse and gone for his gun? Were you plannin' on shootin' him dead or maybe just woundin' him?"

"He wasn't goin' for his gun. I knew he wouldn't. I just wanted to shut up that mouth of his."

"But what if he would have drawn? Just suppose you were wrong. What then?"

"I guess I would have killed him. I, eh . . . never figured he would take me up on it, so I didn't bother with what to do. Say, did Pepper say why she came out today?"

"I reckon by the greeting I got, she was just lonesome."

"What's that supposed to mean?"

"It means I'll be eatin' my supper alone out in the barn tonight!"

Tap turned around in the saddle resting his right hand on Brownie's rump. "Is that pony of yours worn out from last night, or can we pick up the speed?"

"Lead the way. I don't aim to slow down true romance."

They had galloped a couple of miles in the shadowy twilight when Wiley called out. Andrews spun around to see him leap to the ground and stoop to inspect his horse's leg.

"You got problems?" Tap hollered.

"Lamed up. Go on. I'll have to walk him in."

"It's gettin' dark. Can you find your way to the house?"

"I rode through this country last night. No doubt I can do it again. Go on and visit your darlin'."

"I hate to leave you afoot."

"Well, then," Wiley said smiling, "why don't you walk my horse in, and I'll go visit with that yellow-haired girl."

"You sure you're all set?"

"Get out of here, Andrews."

"We'll keep supper warm for you!" Andrews trotted the horse down into a gulch and up the bank on the other side.

For several minutes he listened to the crunch of Brownie's hoofs breaking through the crusty snow.

This is crazy! I can't believe I'm doin' this.

The few scattered trees stood as black sentinels. The snow was taking on a twilight glow as he rode back up into the mountains. In the distance Wiley plodded along leading his horse.

"You get lost, Andrews?"

"Shoot, Wiley, I got to thinkin', and sure enough, I figured you wouldn't find your way to the house. And then just as I'm supposed to be takin' Pepper back to McCurleys', I'll have to ride out here and find you in the dark. So I decided to come find you now and save myself a trip. Hop up here behind me. We'll take it easy, and Brownie can pack us home."

Holding the reins to his own horse, Wiley pulled himself up behind the cantle of Tap's saddle. "Okay, Mr. Andrews, what's the real reason you turned around?"

"It's too cold out here for a man to be afoot. The more I thought about it, the colder I got. The way it was goin', I figured I'd freeze to death just thinkin' about you."

"What about that girl of yours?"

"Well, she don't like driving home in the dark by herself, so I reckon she'll wait for me. I'll get to visit plenty on the way back to McCurleys'."

"I figured she was stayin' at the ranch for a few days."

"Nope. She doesn't stay overnight at the ranch until after the weddin'. We decided a while back that we're doin' it right."

Brownie's slow, labored stride got them into the yard about two hours later. Tap rode right up to the front door.

"I put her rig up in the barn," Wiley reported, "but I don't see any lights on inside."

"Maybe she's back in the kitchen."

Wiley slid off Brownie's rump. Tap climbed down and handed him the reins.

"I'll put up the horses. You go courtin'," Wiley offered.

Tap was pushing through the front door before the word came out of his mouth. "Pepper?"

She's not here!

By the time Wiley entered the house, the lamps were lit, a fire was burning in the fireplace, and Andrews sat at the piano bench reading a letter.

Dear Tap,

It's my fault. I told you I wasn't coming out this week, but I was missing you. I trust you didn't try to take on cattle rustlers by yourself. We really need to talk. Abel Cedar (Suzanne's brother) showed up at the hotel looking for Zachariah Hatcher. I had to tell him about his death—and Miss Cedar's. It was a dreadful experience!

Well, he gave me all of Suzanne's things, even her Bible! However, I gave him the balance of her funds. I know we wanted to get some things for the ranch and buy some more cows, but it really wasn't my money. Now everything I have is rightfully mine. That makes me feel really good. I know it was the right thing to do. I hope you're not disappointed in me.

I think the banker's letter is self-explanatory. Did you know that there was this bank note due on the place? Maybe you have that all covered, and I'm worrying for nothing.

I really can't wait until this is my home, and I never have to drive off and leave you. If you can't get away and come into McCurleys' tomorrow, I'll plan on coming back out on Monday.

Don't worry about the drive back. The banker led the way with his rig.

With much love,
Pepper

"I see her buggy's gone," Wiley reported. "I guess your darlin' got tired of waitin'. She write you a love letter?"

"Huh? Oh, yeah . . . I mean, no," Andrews stammered. "It's just—look at this. I can't believe it! Wiley, you don't happen to have $2,089.45 on you, do you?"

"I got about $9.45. You'll have to cover the rest. What for?"

"I can raise the $80. That only leaves me $2,000 short. Oh, some Ft. Collins banker came by and said the previous owner had a bank note past due. If I don't come up with the funds by January 1, they'll foreclose. The weddin' comin' up, and some joker is threatenin' to take away the ranch. This place is the whole reason I figured now is the time to get married!"

"You mean she's marrying you for your ranch?"

"Eh, no. I—I don't think so. Of course not!"

"Then you'll figure somethin' out. Shoot, for the smile of a pretty lady, a man can determine all sorts of things."

Even the heat of the kitchen and a hot meal failed to fully warm Andrews. After Wiley sauntered out to the tack room for the night, Tap stood staring at the messy bedroom.

I've got half a mind to just leave on my clothes and crawl under the covers . . . but the cold chill is on the inside, so I guess it wouldn't matter.

He hung his Colt on the bedpost and stripped down to his long johns. Turning off the lamp, he pulled the covers up to his chin.

Lord, I'm really tryin'. I want it all to be different. I don't want to bother anyone, and I don't want anyone to bother me.

This ranch doesn't belong to anyone. I want it.

And Pepper.
And some cows and some kids.
I don't want ambushes in the night.
Bankers showin' up demandin' payment.
Neighbors who'd rather shoot me than talk to me.
You know I've been faithful to Pepper. I haven't been drinkin'.
I haven't shot anyone who didn't need shootin'. I'm tryin' to read
up on the Bible and learn all I can. If there's somethin' else I ought
to do, I surely hope You'll show me.

Tap lay on his back and stared up through the window at the stars. Sometime after midnight the stars dimmed, and he fell asleep.

The sound of a wagon and voices in the yard brought him to his feet in the blackness of the room. He hobbled to the front door, pulling on his pants and buckling his holster all at the same time.

People laughing? A woman? Pepper? Who is she with?

He reached the front door just as there was a light knock. The room was dark, but the starlight filtering onto the front porch gave off just enough light for him to tell who it was.

"Selena?"

"Ay, Señor Tapadera. *¿Tiene usted cuartos por las mujeres bonitas y uno hombre grande?*"

"Eh . . . what?"

"You got company, cowboy!" She grinned. Then tossing back her waist-length black hair, she waltzed straight into the front room.

4

D anni Mae?" Andrews stepped aside as a short woman
with thick, wavy brown hair and a tan blanket wrapped
around her shoulders swished into the house behind
Selena.

"Paula? What's going on?" Tap asked the thin woman with a
scar on her chin who followed the others into the darkened front
room. The aroma of heavy French perfume flooded the room.

"We're freezin'—that's what. You don't mind if we borrow
your fire, do you?"

"No . . . eh, no, come in. How did you . . . where's . . ."

Tap had just struck a match to light a lantern near the door
when a girl who looked about sixteen with big, round eyes and
brown hair that hung straight down from a center part scooted
past him.

"Who are you?" he asked, holding the lantern up.

She turned back. In the flicker of the light Tap could see a
turned-up nose, puffy eyes, and tear steaks dried into her cheeks.
"I'm Rocky." Her full lips puckered in a permanent pout.

"Rocky?"

She answered almost in a monotone, "My mama named me
after the mountains."

"Where is your mama?" he questioned.

"Dead. Where's yours?" Her thin shoulders stooped, and she
disappeared into the shadows.

"Danni Mae, where's Stack?" asked Tap.

"He's puttin' the team away in your barn," Danni Mae called. "Tap, do you mind if we stir up your fire?"

"No, no. Make yourself at home," Andrews muttered as he started across the yard toward the barn.

By the time he got there, Wiley had a lamp lit, and he and Stack Lowery were talking in front of a two-horse freight wagon.

"Stack, what in the world's going on?"

"Hey, partner! We were just in the neighborhood and thought we'd stop in for breakfast," the big man joked. Yet his eyes showed very little humor. His voice lowered. "It ain't good, Tap. The dance hall burned to the ground!"

"What happened?"

"Three men rode into Pingree Hill earlier this evenin'. I don't know them too well, but they been doin' business at April's for a couple months, so I didn't think nothin' of it.

"April's been in Denver for over a week, and I was out in the kitchen when the girls started screamin', 'Fire!' By the time I got there, flames was lappin' up the curtains on the north wall and spreadin' toward the bar.

"I yelled at Selena to get the girls and head for the yard. Then I ran upstairs to make sure the rooms was empty. I had to carry Rocky out to the porch and then ran back in to help a couple of the boys toss water on the fire. Well, that pump was pert' near froze up, so we was lucky to toss a bucket or two. Meanwhile, the flames had shot right up to the second floor, and I told the boys it was time for us to get out, too.

"I covered my mouth and busted into April's room. I figured on grabbin' the cash box, shotgun, and a few pieces of her jewelry. But the cash box was busted open, and all the money was gone. Not only that, the east wall was on fire."

"It spread that fast?"

"It was a separate fire."

"So you figure the dance hall fire was just to divert you?"

"Yep. The girls were huddlin' on the porch, and they said all three of them hombres hightailed it to the south the minute I ran back inside. I tried to settle 'em down over in the barn, but they was freezin' and worried. That little one, Rocky, jist knew that they would circle back and shoot us all. I hitched up the team and tried to figure where to take them. Snow's closed roads off to the east, and we didn't want to follow the outlaws, so we headed west to the closest place that would have a fire and some shelter."

"These men—was there a big one named Karl and another maybe, eh, Hank?"

Stack stopped unhitching the team and looked at Andrews. "And Bufe—that's them! You know 'em?"

"I had a showdown with them about noon yesterday. They were runnin' some Rafter R beef through my place. That youngest one was shot in the leg."

"That's the one that was missin'!"

"You want to go out after them now?" Tap asked.

"To tell you the truth," Stack said rubbing his big, callused hands together, "I need to warm up, git a bite to eat, and catch a nap. I ain't goin' to be no help if I fall asleep in the saddle."

"We can start after them first thing tomorrow, but it might be rough to catch 'em."

Stack's squared jaw looked chiseled in stone. "At least we got to try, Tap. Most of that money belonged to those girls. All they got is what they carried with 'em. That dance hall burned like a dead fir tree in July."

"Well . . . when you and Wiley get those horses stalled, come on over. I'll go see if I can stir up something for everyone to eat. It ought to be breakin' daylight soon."

When he entered the house, Selena was in the rocking chair with the gray and white cat in her lap, her long black hair spread across her shoulders like a shawl. Danni Mae came over to Tap. He had never noticed how deep the wrinkles were around her tired-looking eyes.

"How's Pepper?" she asked.

"She was here yesterday, but I missed seeing her," Tap reported. "I was chasin' some rustlers off my place. Probably the same bunch that hit April's."

"How are the plans for the wedding?"

"Everything's on schedule. She's got every minute planned out. Say, you'll still be able to sing, won't you?"

Danni Mae took a deep breath and sighed. "I surely hope so, but who knows now? I really don't know what we're goin' to do, Tap. We don't have two dollars among the whole lot of us."

"Me and Stack will ride out tomorrow and get your money back. Right now I'll see if I can stir up some food. Pepper cooked a few things that me and Wiley didn't finish."

"Wiley?"

"Oh, he's a friend of mine stayin' at the ranch a few days."

"I'll help you. I surely don't want Stack to cook the eggs." Danni Mae raised her eyebrows and scooted past him into the kitchen.

By the time the clear night sky turned a light gray, the crowd at Tap's house had crammed around the big front room table scraping tin plates piled with steaming potatoes, beef, and eggs. No one talked much, and the girls still looked tired and stunned. Rocky sat by the fire refusing to eat.

"Ladies," Tap began, "there's only one bedroom in this house. It's a mess, but you all are welcome to it. Just kick my stuff out of there and make that bedroom home."

"Now don't that beat all?" Selena leaned over the table toward Tap. "That blonde bobcat's down at McCurleys', and I'm here in Señor Tapadera's *alcoba!*"

"All four of us will be in the bedroom!" Danni Mae insisted.

The women left the three men sitting at the table drinking coffee.

"Well, Mr. Lowery, what about it? You still want to wait 'til tomorrow mornin'?" Tap asked.

"I've been thinkin'," the tall, strong-shouldered man drawled. "We can't move in on you and Pepper like this. Maybe I ought to take these girls to Laramie City. Yummie Jackson has a little hotel up there, and he owes me a favor or two. Then I could ride down to Denver and find April and maybe stop off and notify the sheriff."

"These boys could be anywhere from El Paso to San Diego by then. Look . . . leave the ladies here at the ranch for a while. Let's ride out tomorrow and see if we cut their trail. The sheriff won't come over the pass 'til spring to help the dance-hall girls, and you know it."

"But I only planned on spendin' the night. You think Pepper would mind all of us camping out at the ranch?" Stack asked.

"She was countin' on you playin' the piano and Danni Mae

singin' at the weddin'. If you all move off to Laramie City and miss that event, it would break her heart. She invited everyone of you to attend, didn't she?"

"All but Selena." Stack raised his dark, bushy eyebrows. "The last time the two of them was in the same room, they were yankin' hair, gougin' eyes, and pullin' knives."

"Oh, Pepper's over that now! It won't be any bother. You can roll out of here right after the wedding. It'll be over by noon, you know. You'll still make it to Wyomin' before Christmas."

Wiley pulled out his barlow knife and picked his teeth. "Now I was thinkin'," he said grinning, "I don't know those boys like you do, and I reckon the two of ya probably had more experience with a gun, so if you figure someone ought to hang around the ranch and protect the womenfolk . . . well, I could."

Tap glanced at Stack and winked. "Wiley, which one you got your eye set on?"

Wiping his mouth with his dark green bandanna, Wiley leaned over the table and spoke in a low voice. "That short one with the curly, brown hair looks like a regular belle. Is she called Danni Mae?"

"Good choice." Stack grinned. "She don't carry no knife."

"The others carry knives?"

"Yep. But Danni Mae just carries a pistol," Tap joshed.

Stack gulped down the rest of his coffee and waved the cup at Wiley. "But don't worry none. It's just a little two-shot .32. It won't do much damage unless it hits something vital!"

Both Tap and Stack roared.

"You aren't speakin' for the brand now, are you?" Wiley pressed.

"I don't rightly know what they carry on any given evenin', but every one of them girls can sure enough take care of herself," Stack assured him.

Tap felt a draft. He rolled down his sleeves and buttoned them. "It would be good to have one of us here . . . just in case those outlaws double back or Fightin' Ed comes raidin' again."

Wiley slapped the table with the open palm of his left hand. "That's exactly what I was thinkin'."

"Stack, Wiley's fixin' up the tack room as a bunkhouse. You go on out and get some sleep. I've got to ride down to McCurleys' and try to catch up with a banker. There's a little misunderstandin' about an old bank loan. I'll be back tonight, and we'll light out by daybreak tomorrow. I figure if we can't find their trail in three days, we won't find it at all."

Tap left the Triple Creek Ranch by midmorning. Selena, Danni Mae, Paula, and Rocky occupied the house while Stack and Wiley bunked out next to the woodstove in the barn. The low orange sun offered little hope for heat, and Tap's teeth chattered as he bounced along with Onespot's unsteady gait.

He'd like someone lighter in the saddle, but ol' Brownie needed a little rest.

There's nothin' on my copy of the deed that says anything about a bank loan. Maybe he's got the wrong ranch. Maybe he's a huckster out workin' the small-time ranchers. I heard about that fellow down near Durango who had 'em all convinced to pay him off.

I need to get Wade Eagleman to look into this! He's a lawyer. He'll know what to do.

I can't go to Denver! Every dream I've had in the past four weeks has been about being in Denver and not being able to get back to the ranch for the wedding.

I'll ride up north to Laramie City and send him a telegram. . . . But Stack said that gang headed south.

The bones in his feet and hands ached by the time McCurleys' came into view, and Tap looked forward to the big fireplace in the parlor and a hot cup of coffee. He pulled his saddle from Onespot, turned the black pony out in the corrals, and then hustled over to the hotel. Other than the barn and a few outbuildings, the hotel was the only place for miles.

Bob McCurley met him at the front door wearing a heavy red flannel shirt.

"Seen you puttin' up Onespot. Figured you knew your way around the barn." McCurley hooked his thumbs into his suspenders.

"The amount of time I spend here I ought to rent stall space."

"Shoot, me and the missus sort of figure you're marryin' into the family. Mama's just about adopted that Pepper of yours."

"Well, where is that yellow-haired girl?"

"Come on in and take some dinner." McCurley tossed his mus-
cled arm around Tap's shoulder. "She ought to be back by the time
you get the road chill out of your bones."

"She's not here?" Tap tugged off his deerskin gloves.

"Nope. Mrs. Franklin sent word that she was going to leave
tomorrow to go to Ogden to have that baby of hers at her
mother's. So she needed Pepper to come out and get the final fit-
tin', or whatever, on that weddin' dress. She said she'd be back by
three at the latest."

"Well, I'll just take you up on dinner." Tap tried to shrug off
the disappointment. "Is that Ft. Collins banker around?"

"He left his rig here and took the morning stage east."

"Looks like I traveled all mornin' for nothin'."

"Pepper will be back later. Now come on and get something
to eat."

Tap jammed his coat on a hook by the door. "Did you hear
about the dance hall over at Pingree Hill burnin' down?"

"You don't say! Ain't that where Pepper—I mean, didn't she . . ."

"Come on in and sit a spell with me, Bob. I'll tell you about it
over some meat and potatoes."

Tap and Bob McCurley talked about the fire, the rustlers, and
the banker's demand for loan repayment for the next two hours.
The only thing he didn't mention was the fact that the girls now
occupied the ranch. They were sitting in the parlor drinking coffee when McCurley finally had to excuse himself to do chores.

For the next hour Tap talked hunting with a dry goods drummer,
but mainly he paced the floor. It was almost dark when a man in a
buckboard full of sacks of oats rolled into the yard. Tap watched the
man unload six 120-pound sacks and hand Bob McCurley a note.

McCurley strolled over to Tap. "Pratt Moore brought me this
note from Pepper. He rode in from the Franklin place. You take a
look at it. I ain't got my readin' glasses."

Tap unfolded the heavy beige paper and glanced at Pepper's
familiar scrawl. McCurley hovered about his shoulder.

Andrews's eyes followed line after line on the letter. He turned to catch a little more daylight. "She says the Franklin woman broke early and begged her to stay the night and help with the delivery."

"She ain't comin' back tonight?"

"Nope. 'Course, she didn't know I was goin' to be visitin' today anyway."

"We'll find some room. You jist spend the night and talk to her in the mornin'."

"Bob, I promised I'd help Stack track down those men. I'll have to ride back to the ranch tonight. I'll leave her a note and explain things . . . I guess. This surely is a strange way to court a woman—just writin' back and forth and never seein' each other."

"Sort of reminds you of Hatcher and that Cedar woman, don't it?" McCurley remarked.

Tap tugged on his jacket and scratched out a note at the small table next to the coat rack by the front door of the hotel.

Pepper,

I missed the banker, so I'm goin' to contact Wade Eagleman in Denver and see what he can do about that matter of the loan against the ranch. There's nothing about it on my copy of Hatcher's deed.

April's dance hall burnt down (Mr. Mac can fill you in), and I've got to go help Stack Lowery track the men who did it. Stack's countin' on me, and a man's got to stick by his friends. Don't worry about me. I faced this bunch before. I'll swing by McCurleys' when we're through.

Suzanne's money would have been a real help with this bank loan business. But we both sort of knew it wasn't ours in the first place. We'll figure somethin' out. I'm not goin' to lose the ranch!

I miss you like crazy.

Tap

P.S. I'll bet the dress looks right handsome!

The moon was not much more than a thin slice when darkness hit, and the stars dotted the coal black sky. Tap tried to find warmth in his thoughts of Pepper, but his feet, hands, and face felt frozen before he and Onespot reached the river crossing halfway to the ranch.

The steam from his breath quickly froze and turned his mustache icy white. Onespot's small stride seemed more sluggish than ever, and the miles throbbed by slowly.

Lord, I know the girls aren't exactly paragons of public virtue, but they deserve better than this. And for the life of me, I can't think of anyone on earth, except for me and Stack, who would help them. I know the Good Book says to help the widows and orphans, and these girls . . . well, they're somewhere in between. Somebody's got to look after them, Lord.

The lamps burned bright behind the curtains of the front room at the ranch house when Tap Andrews rode into the yard. The barn was dark and silent as he groomed the black gelding. He could hear someone playing the piano as he approached the front porch. His pounding boot heels and jingling spurs were drowned out by the noise and laughter from inside.

He started to knock on the door.

Wait! It's my house! I can't be intrudin'!

The music stopped when he walked through the doorway.

"Welcome to the funeral!" Stack greeted him from the piano bench. Selena sat next to him. Danni Mae and Wiley hovered near the fireplace. Rocky sat motionless in the rocker staring blankly into the glowing coals. Sal, the gray and white cat, perched on her lap. Paula Sangtree sat at the kitchen table with a blanket wrapped around her, sewing her dress.

"A funeral?" Tap slung his coat on a hook and scooted to the fire.

"Yep. Tonight we are buryin' the dance hall! Say—how's that Pepper girl?" Stack asked.

"Well . . . I didn't see her."

Selena sidled over to Tap and slipped her arm in his. "Did she run out on you, *caballero?*"

"Oh, she got tied up deliverin' a baby for the lady who's sewing her weddin' dress."

"That will be useful knowledge for her to have," Selena teased.

An hour later Tap, Stack, and Wiley hunkered across the frozen snow to the barn. Stoking the woodstove in the tack room, the three huddled close for warmth.

"What's the schedule in the mornin'?" Stack asked.

Wiley rubbed his hands together close to the fire. "You still want me to stay with the women?"

"Nope."

Wiley grinned broadly. "I figured that was too good to be true."

"I need you to ride to Laramie City and send two telegrams. You're the only one who can ride up and cross the Rafter R without bein' shot at."

"What kind of telegrams?"

"One to April notifying her of the fire and that the girls will be at the ranch until December 22. The other to a lawyer friend in Denver. I'm hopin' he can help me with the bank note. I'll scribble them out for you."

Sometime during the night dark, heavy clouds slid into the Colorado sky between the North Platte River and the Medicine Bow Mountains. Sometime during the night Tap thought he heard sounds of a woman crying in the ranch house. And sometime during the night the fire in the stove went out.

"You're movin' around like an old man," Stack mumbled as Tap hobbled around the potbellied stove trying to revive the fire.

"Some parts of me feel older than others. You know what I mean?"

Stack crawled out from under the blankets and began to pull on his tall, black stove-top boots. "Yep. Ever' knife wound, ever' broken bone, ever' scrap of lead you carry has a way of remindin' you of your past sins, don't they?"

"Well, at least it ain't snowin' yet," Wiley interrupted as he came waltzing back into the barn.

"You're up early. You been out huntin'?" Stack teased.

"Eh . . . no. I just thought I'd check on the womenfolk."

"Mighty kind of ya." Tap winked at Stack. "You'll hurry back from Laramie City, won't you, Wiley?"

"Oh, yes, sir. You can count on me to git right back to the ranch."

"That's what I figured."

Tap started to saddle up Brownie, but he stopped and walked over to Stack. "Hey, partner, did I hear one of the gals cryin' last night? Is there some problem I don't know about?"

Stack nodded and continued to saddle his own horse. "Yeah. I heard it too. It was Rocky."

"How old is she?"

"Says she's eighteen, but I got my doubts." Stack shrugged.

"What's she doin' in the hurdy-gurdy business?"

"From what I hear, she got pregnant a few years back, and the boy ran out on her. She ended up with some hack doctor giving her an abortion. She started likin' laudanum to relieve the pain, and . . . you know how that stuff is, Tap. It's poison. Well, April's been helpin' her come off the stuff. She'd only give her a little at night to get to sleep. But it got burnt up. So I guess she's feelin' mighty poorly without that laudanum."

"She's a pretty, little thing. She doesn't have to do this," Tap observed.

"That's what I tried to tell her. You might mention it to her, Tap. She might believe you. She sees herself as a little lower than a snake and figures everyone else looks at her that way too. I worry about her more than all the others combined."

"She's the kind that don't last long in this business," Tap added.

"She's the kind that don't last long in this world," Stack corrected.

By keeping a steady pace, Tap and Stack reached the still-smoldering ruins of April's dance hall in the middle of the afternoon. They rode south, stopping at several ranch houses to inquire about four men on the run. It was almost dark when they found a rancher who had spotted three men camping near Red Springs the previous night.

"They had their carbines on their laps and surely seemed happy to see me ride on," the man reported. "The big man did all the talkin'."

"That would be Karl," Andrews surmised.

He and Stack spent a cold night at the camp near Red Springs, and early the next morning they found the trail of three riders slanting off to the southwest.

"You think that's them?"

"Well, if you were swinging around toward Rico Springs, wouldn't you cut this trail?"

"Reckon so."

"Besides, if we can't find them, at least we'll be closer to McCurleys'."

"You figurin' on stoppin' by and seein' Pepper before goin' back to the ranch?"

"Yep."

The clouds hung low all day, and the west wind seemed to be pressing them tighter against the continental divide to the east. Tap could no longer remember the last time his bones had been warm. They hit the road that linked Rico Springs and Kare Kremmling's store at dusk. Shortly afterward they rode south into town. On the well-traveled road all signs of the three men they followed were obliterated.

Isolation was the only reason for Rico Springs's existence, and that feature attracted an assortment of eccentrics—those hiding from the law and those just plain hiding. The buildings occupied one block on either side of the north and south road. There was no post office, no stage stop, no church, no jail, and no houses—to speak of.

Hidden behind the unpainted false-front facades were a mercantile, a grocery store, a livery, a hotel that consisted of one huge log room full of wooden bunks, and six gambling hall saloons.

"How come Rico Springs doesn't have a dance hall, Stack? Some hurdy-gurdy operator is missing a lot of customers."

"They had one," Stack replied. "Within a week every girl was either shot, knifed, or ran off. After that, none of the girls would come close to this place."

"Sounds like a perfect spot for these rustlers that burnt down April's."

Stack pulled off his gloves and blew steam into his hands. "What's our plan now? This bunch knows both of us on sight, and it's too cold to stand out here in the dark and wait for them to wander by."

"We don't even know if they're in town. We'll just poke around real careful and see if we can stir something up. You figure you know most of the boys up here?"

"I'd figure half the town's been at April's one time or another."

"Then let me lead the way, and you come in about ten steps behind me."

"Don't kill 'em until I find out where the girls' money is," Stack cautioned.

"Kill 'em? I don't have any intention of killin' 'em."

"No, and you didn't plan on killin' Jordan Beckett and that bunch."

"They didn't leave me any choice."

"And how about Victor Barranca?"

"I didn't kill Vic. It was the deputy. Remember?"

"What I'm sayin' is that when you're around in a gunfight, Andrews, people have a habit of dyin'."

"I've never really noticed that. Are you saying I have a character flaw?"

"What I'm sayin' is I want to get the girls' money back and deliver you to your yellow-haired darlin', so don't plan on takin' on the entire population of Rico Springs at the same time."

Tap's spurs jingled his path to the tall, narrow wooden doors that led into The Bucket. The aroma of smoke and the smell of cheap alcohol reminded him of a thousand such places across the Western frontier. It took him a little less than four steps to know that none of the rustlers were in the room. He strolled through the stares and sidled up to the bar made of packing crates and planks.

A man wearing two bullet belts and two revolvers greeted him from behind the counter. "Evenin', mister. You lookin' for somethin' to fill your belly?"

"I'm really lookin' for old Karl and Hank and that bunch. Have they been in tonight?"

The man studied Tap up and down. "I don't reckon I've seen you in here before."

Tap stared right at the man's weak gray eyes. "And I don't reckon you answered my question."

Suddenly the man hollered out to the rest of the men in the room, "Any of you boys know a man named Karl?"

Most heads shook no, but Tap noticed that their hands went straight for their revolver handles and rested there.

In the momentary hush, Tap spoke up. "If any of you ever meet a man named Karl, tell him I need to talk to him about Jimmy Ray. The boy's carryin' lead and not doin' too well. I thought Karl would want to know."

Almost in unison, hands relaxed and slipped off the walnut and pearl handles of .44s and .45s.

"Is Jimmy Ray goin' to pull through, mister?" A man at the end of the homemade bar began to grill him.

"If they kin get that bullet out."

"Where'd he get shot?" The question sounded more like a test than a sincere inquiry.

Stack sauntered into The Bucket and leaned against the wall near the front door. "The bullet's stuck in there above the knee in his right leg."

"Well, I'll be! Who done it?"

"I heard some old rancher up on the border who didn't like losin' bovines."

"Some men git right touchy about that, I reckon. Listen, I know Karl, Hank, and Bufe. If I run across 'em, I'll tell 'em you was askin' for 'em. You goin' to be around town awhile?"

"Maybe. Are there any square card games in this town?"

"Not many." The man laughed and downed his drink. "Think I'll promenade up the street and see if I kin find me some hot supper."

You're goin' straight to Karl!

The bartender wiped his hands on his dirty white apron and grumbled, "You drinkin' or not?"

"Right now I'd just like a hot cup of coffee to warm these bones."

"Coffee's over on the woodstove. Help yourself. Toss a nickel in that tin cup, and you kin drink it all night. And, listen, I heard

you say you was lookin' for a card game. That table at the back
will have a game around nine. You can probably buy in there."

"Is it an honest game?"

"Well, it's about as honest as you can git in Rico Springs."

Tap walked toward the woodstove and glanced at Stack as he
poured a cup of coffee. Lowery signaled with his eyes and head
that he would go up the street checking out the other businesses.

Meandering over to the empty corner table, Tap took a chair
with his back against the wall. From his vantage point he could
see almost everyone in the room, but the stove made it difficult
for someone just entering the room to observe him. Stack had
already slipped out.

He had been there only a few minutes when a short man in a
wide Mexican hat burst through the front door, downed two
quick drinks at the bar, and headed straight for Tap's table.

Coffee in his left hand, Andrews slipped his right hand down
to the walnut grip on his Colt.

"Mister, you here for a game of cards?"

Tap noticed that the right half of the man's face was permanently blackened while the left half was sort of a cold pink color.
The man obviously had a glass right eye. "I heard there might be
one later on." Tap nodded. "You plannin' on playin'?"

"Playin'? I'm plannin' on winnin'!" the man roared. "My
name's Half-Beard. And yourself?"

"Call me Tap. Looks like you took a pretty good blow with
some black powder."

"Durin' the war. The dang musket blew up in my face. I lost an
eye, eardrum, and half my face, but at least I still have my good
looks!" The man roared again. "Kin I buy you a drink?"

"No thanks. I'm still drinkin' this boiled coffee."

"Well, shoot, you kin buy me a drink!" He laughed and yelled
for the bartender to bring a bottle. "After I rake in a few dollars
here, I think I'll ride on up to Pingree Hill. You ever been to that
hurdy-gurdy house they got up there? There are some of the purdiest girls north of Denver. They got a yellow-haired girl up there . . ."

Tap realized that he had already pulled his revolver halfway out of the holster and had his finger poised on the trigger. He shoved the Colt back in and tried to relax his grip.

"Not any more, they don't!"

"Wh-hat?" the man spat.

"It burnt down a couple of nights ago."

"You don't say! How'd it happen?"

"Some bunch decided to rob April and the girls at the dance hall, so they burnt the place down for a diversion."

"That ain't right! Depriving them girls of their place of, eh, work. You know who done it?"

"Got my suspicions, but I can't say just yet."

"Burned clean to the ground, you say?"

"Yep."

"No more April's. . . . Say, where'd them girls go?"

"I heard they were on their way to Wyomin'."

"Don't that beat all? Country without a dance hall—it's a lonely place, ain't it? How about that yellow-haired girl? She go up to Wyomin', too?"

"The one called Pepper?"

"Yeah, that's her! A firecracker, she is. I once seen her get the drop on old Jordan Beckett—jist a week or two before he died. There ain't many in this country that ever got the drop on old Beckett . . . exceptin' that Arizony gunslinger that finally gunned him down. What about that yellow-haired girl?"

"Didn't you hear? She's marryin' that Arizona gunslinger."

"No foolin'? Mister, I'm glad you told me that! That's one man I surely don't aim to ever sit at the same table with. No, sir."

"I hear he's as tough as old Stuart Brannon," Tap added trying hard not to smile.

"I heard that, too, but I don't rightly believe it." Half-Beard looked around the room for a spittoon. "What time did you say the action's goin' to commence around here anyway?"

Out of the corner of his eye Tap spied the man called Hank push open the door and scope the room. "I reckon it's just about to get started."

5

The unshaven man stomped over to the bartender and waded into an animated conversation. The man's gun was hung low on his hip for all to see below his jacket, but Tap knew it was too low to be a real threat.

Tap spoke softly to Half-Beard. "Think I'll get a refill of coffee. It's as bitter as sin, but it's hot. You need a cup?"

"Coffee? Shoot, I ain't got drunk enough for coffee—yet!" he boomed and poured himself another shot from the amber unlabeled bottle in front of him. He spilled a few drops on his dirty fingers, which he promptly lapped up.

The bartender pointed toward the big, round table in the back just as Tap slipped behind the woodstove and refilled his tin cup. Standing in the shadows, he watched Hank stalk to the back of the saloon, his right hand resting on the handle of the revolver in its black, slick, concho-studded leather holster.

Mister, you'll be dead before you ever get that high enough to squeeze off a shot.

"Hey, old man! Are you the one who claims to have a message from Jimmy Ray?" Hank's voice sounded high and taut.

Half-Beard looked up and glanced around the room. "You talkin' to me?"

"What's it look like?" Hank growled.

"Do I have a message from who?"

Hank drew his revolver halfway out of the holster. "You heard me, mister!" he barked.

Half-Beard ignored the man and poured himself another drink, wiping his mouth on his canvas coat sleeve. Just as Hank got his gun out of the holster, Tap stepped up behind him. Grabbing Hank by the greasy coat collar, he jammed his own Colt in the man's back, shielding his gun from all in the room except Half-Beard.

"Just lay that hog leg of yours nice and gentle on the table and sit down, Hank. It's time to talk!"

Bending his neck around to an awkward position, Hank exclaimed, "You! Why, I ought to—"

"You do remember that I don't hesitate to shoot a man, don't you? I'm sure Jimmy Ray hasn't forgot. Unless you dumped him along the trail and sold his horse and saddle." Tap dragged the man to the back wall and shoved him into an empty chair. Then he sat next to Hank, never loosing his grip on the collar or the .44. From this vantage, Tap's gun couldn't be seen by anyone, and he could still keep an eye on the whole room. No one even glanced back at them.

"I see you two have met before." Half-Beard nodded. "If you plan on pullin' that trigger, I'd like to move away a tad. This here's my only coat, and I don't aim to get it all blood-splattered so early in the season."

"Well, now, that depends upon old Hank here. If he tries somethin' dumb, I'll be forced to send a bullet right about—there!" He jabbed Hank in the back with the pistol barrel. "I'd guess the bullet would pass clean through and hit that mirror on the far wall. But you know how it is. If it hits a bone or a vital organ, why, it could just squirt out any old direction. Now are you plannin' on doin' somethin' dumb, Hank?"

Hank's weak, narrow eyes glared at Tap. "You ain't got a chance in hades of gettin' out of here."

"You don't plan on stoppin' me, do ya?"

"I got a room full of friends," Hank panted. "All I got to do is yell."

"Well, make sure it's good and loud 'cause the second you start screamin', there'll be a loud explosion from this Colt, and I'd surely want them to understand what you was sayin' since it would be your last words on earth."

"What are you doin' here anyway? We didn't take none of your cows, and you know it," Hank protested, glancing over his shoulder at the cocked .44 and Tap's finger on the trigger. "Ease your finger back, mister. That thing could go off by accident."

"Hank, this Colt has never, ever gone off by accident. Now where's the money from the dance hall?"

"Did he say you was a rancher?" Half-Beard interrupted. "Where's your place?"

"Up on the Wyomin' border," Tap answered. "A nice, little spread between the Medicine Bows and the North Platte."

"He ain't no rancher. He's an Arizona gunslinger!" Hank murmured. "Why, he shot Jimmy Ray outright and intends to do the same to me if he kin get away with it!"

"An Arizona gunslinger?" Half-Beard choked back his drink, cleared his throat, and shoved his hat back. "You the one who shot Jordan Beckett when he had a gun drawn on ya?"

"Yep."

Half-Beard rubbed his face with his right hand, revealing half a trigger finger missing. "Word around Denver is you took on Barranca and Dillard."

"They were fools."

"They were mean fools! Well, I'll be! Say, are you the one who's marryin' that yellow-haired girl?"

"Yep."

Half-Beard took the big bottle by the neck and chugged down another swallow. "Hope you didn't take no insult in what I said earlier about that purdy yellow-haired girl. I surely didn't mean to rile ya none, no, sir."

"No offense, Half-Beard. I only thought about shootin' you for a minute or two, but that passed quickly." Tap smiled slyly.

"Well, sir . . ." Half-Beard's face flushed from a combination of fear and alcohol. "I think maybe it's time I should step outside and git me a little fresh air—that is, if it don't inflame ya none."

"You're goin' to come back and play a little poker, aren't you?" Tap inquired.

"With the dance hall at Pingree Hill burned down, I was thinkin' . . . well, maybe I'll ride up toward Leadville."

"Don't go too far for a while. This old boy is one of them that burned April's down."

"You don't say!"

"He's lyin'! I was there tryin' to put the fire out! Ask the girls. Ask that big piano player."

"That's a good idea." Andrews kept his grip on the man's coat. "Half-Beard, go down the line and see if you can find Stack Lowery. He'll be the tallest man in Rico Springs. You know, he's the piano player from April's."

Hank tried to turn around and look at Andrews. "He's here in town?" he gasped.

"Yeah, isn't that a romp? Me and Hank will just sit right here and wait for Stack. Then I'll let the boys in the room decide what will happen to you. I don't figure they'll be real tickled to learn you destroyed the dance hall."

"I don't believe you. You're bluffin' me. That piano player ain't in Rico Springs."

"Well, I believe him. I'll send Lowery your way, mister," Half-Beard promised. He stood to his feet, steadied himself, and waddled toward the front door, tossing a coin at the bartender.

The roar of the crowd in the saloon subsided. Several men now stared their way.

Tap looked up, smiled, and called out, "Me and ol' Hank here is just settlin' up some debts. Seems he took a little money that didn't belong to him."

"He's a filthy liar! I didn't take nothin' of his!" Hank shouted. "Go get Karl, boys. He'll settle the whole thing!"

"Mister," a deep voice from across the room boomed, "Hank's a regular around here. You better lay down that gun right now!"

"I'm surely glad he's a friend of yours. That way I know you won't want to cause him any mortal injury. Ya see, the first gun yanked from the holster, and I'll pull this trigger."

He leaned over to Hank. "Now we'll find out who your friends are. Anyone who grabs for his pistol obviously wants you dead."

"W-wait, boys, wait!" Hank's words ran together as he talked. "Wait'll-Karl-getshere. This-man'll-shootme-fursure."

"Old Hank is a little nervous, isn't he?"

"How much money does he owe ya?" Another voice rolled across the now-silent saloon.

"Well, that's the thing. It isn't me he robbed. Hank and a couple others plundered the girls at April's and then burned the place down! And I figure those purdy dancin' girls deserve their money back. What do you boys think?"

"He's crazy! The only thing we did is try to put the fire out! He's just mad 'cause we was on his ranch. He shot Jimmy Ray point-blank and is tryin' to do the same to me!"

The front door opened, then closed quickly, but no one entered the saloon.

"There ain't goin' to be any shootin' in here tonight!" The bartender swung a shotgun out from behind the bar and waved it at Tap and Hank. "I don't give two bits who kills who, but you ain't doin' it in here! Git out that back door, or I'll pull the trigger and cut you both in two."

A whiskey bottle crashed into the back of the bartender's head, sending a blast from the shotgun into the ceiling. The man crumpled to the floor in a litter of broken glass and spilled liquor.

"It's too dang cold to go outside and watch a gunfight!" someone called. "Go ahead, mister, make your play."

Tap couldn't tell which man had cold-cocked the bartender.

"He's the one that gunned down Jordan Beckett," Hank hollered. "I heard him say so himself!"

"Lots of us were friends of Beckett!" another shouted.

"I'll give fifty dollars to the man who guns him down!" Hank screamed. Sweat rolled down the back of his neck.

"That's a lot of money, boys," Tap pointed out. "Where do you suppose Hank got that kind of money? He's spendin' your dance hall money!"

A skinny man at the bar, his right hand resting on a revolver tucked into his belt, glanced at the back door, then over to Tap, then back at the door.

At that moment Tap jerked Hank to the left toward the door

and kicked over the table just as Bufe barreled in, pistol in hand. Shoved from the back, Hank stumbled into Bufe and caused the gun-toting outlaw to fall to the floor, firing wildly.

"I shot my foot!" Bufe screamed. "Git off me, Hank. I shot my foot!"

Tap fired one shot at a row of bottles behind the makeshift bar. In the cover of gun smoke so thick he could no longer see the other saloon patrons, he dove out the back door just as bullets began to fly.

The shock of ice-cold air on his lungs combined with the acid taste of gun smoke caused him to cough as he tumbled out the back door. He rolled to his feet.

"Sounds a little unhealthy in there!" said someone standing in the shadows.

"Stack?"

"Say, Andrews, do you need any help, or is everything under control?"

"You plannin' on standin' out here and waitin' for them to kill me?"

"I just got here."

"Let's get out of the alley!" Tap called.

"You find out where the girls' money is?"

"Eh . . . no. How about you?"

"Nope."

They ran behind the buildings. Tap kicked out the empty brass cartridge and shoved another bullet into the chamber of his .44. Several more shots rang out inside the saloon.

"What are they shootin' at now?"

"The smoke, I guess."

"Who got shot?"

"Bufe shot himself in the toe. That's all I know."

"You think they're carryin' the money?"

"Karl's got to be the one. He must be in town somewhere."

"If I were him, I'd catch a saddle and ride," Stack offered.

"The livery?"

"That's my guess."

"Stack, you go north, and I'll go south. Don't let him get out of town."

"We better do it pronto before the air clears at The Bucket."

Tap sprinted through the crusty snow, circled the building, and came back onto the main road. There were no street lights in Rico Springs. The only light glowed through the windows and doorways. A crowd had gathered at the front door of The Bucket Saloon.

His boot heel hit the hard-packed snow of the road as his feet slipped out from under him. Tap slammed headfirst into the icy roadway. Half-stunned for a minute from the fall, he rolled over on his back to try to catch his breath. In the dark he groped to recover his revolver as a horse galloped toward him.

He's running right over the top of me!

Tap screamed, "Whoa! Whoa, boy!"

The horse reared up three feet from Andrews, who managed to roll out from under the slashing hooves just as the rider tumbled to the shadowy roadway.

Karl?

Tap lunged at the fallen man and met the cold, hard steel of a rifle barrel as it smashed into his right ear. He dove to the left to avoid another blow and could hear nothing but a loud ringing in his ear. Blood trickled down his neck.

Tap kicked wildly at the man's leg. His boot toe caught the big man just below the knee, and the rifle dropped to the ground as the man collapsed to the ice.

A lantern-toting crowd was forming around them. Karl pulled his revolver. The clinched right cross caught Karl hard in the chin, and Tap could feel the skin over his knuckles tear. Karl stumbled back, dropped the revolver, and grasped his chin.

Both circled inside the screaming crowd, looking for position, catching their breath. For several minutes they traded punch for punch straight up. Each struggled to stay on his feet.

Finally, Tap lunged but caught a knee right below the rib cage. He tackled Karl on the way down, gasping for breath, but found he couldn't lift his arm. The big man in the coat made from a four-point Hudson blanket battered his massive fist into Tap's side and broke free. Both men struggled to stand and tottered in the darkness.

The crowd jeered and cheered, but Tap could hear nothing but a pulsating chime in his ear. Karl pounced at him. Tap stepped aside, locked his hands, and crashed them into the back of Karl's head. The big man slipped to the ice, but he grabbed Tap on the way down and managed to land a half-strength blow to the chin that made Tap's teeth rattle.

He yanked a handful of Karl's oily hair and, pulling it down hard, slammed the man's head into the frozen roadway. The third blow to the ice knocked Karl unconscious, and Tap raised up on his hands and knees. His chest heaved, and his ears rang as he crawled across the packed snow and retrieved his revolver and dirty gray hat. Struggling to his feet, he glanced around at the crowd of men. Most seemed to be shouting and passing money back and forth, but he couldn't hear anything but the noise in his ear.

Andrews was startled when a rider leading a horse broke through the crowd and reined up next to him.

"Stack?" He couldn't even hear his own voice. Stack Lowery slid off the horse. His mouth was moving, but Tap couldn't understand the words. "I can't hear you, Stack!"

"Don't yell!"

"What?"

"Quit yellin' and mount up," Stack insisted.

"What?"

Walking around to Andrews's left ear, Stack cupped his hand and shouted, "Mount up and let's ride before they all change their minds!"

"What?" Tap hollered. "Mount up?"

Stack nodded his head and pointed to Brownie.

"What about the girls' money?"

Lowery's big, callused hand slapped over Tap's mouth. "Mount up now!"

Tap limped over to Brownie and lifted his left hand to the saddle horn. He tried several times but failed to get his left leg up into the stirrup. Stack grabbed him by the back of his britches and his coat collar and shoved him into the saddle. The big piano player swung up on his own horse and, with a kick of the spurs, both men rode south into the darkness along the slick mountain roadway.

The cloud cover hid the moon and stars, but the snow on the ground reflected enough light for them to distinguish the road from the black shadows.

I can't hear. That blow to the ear . . . What's goin' on? My head's still bleedin'. My knuckle's busted. Feels like I got a broken rib. I've been shot and never hurt this bad! Lord, You've got to stop that ringing.

He yanked off his bandanna and tried mopping his forehead and ear. Even though most of his face was freezing, his right ear felt like it was on fire. He was starting to get dizzy. He seized the saddle horn with both hands.

Lord, somethin's wrong here. . . . I'm not goin' to fall off!

Tap set his feet deep in the stirrups, tried to lock his knees into Brownie's flanks, and resorted to grabbing onto the forks of the saddle. He slumped forward but tried to push himself back up straight. Right after that the reins flopped to the deep brown mane of the horse. But Tap didn't feel them slip from his gloved left hand.

The Arizona sun crackled with heat as he blinked his eyes open. His lips felt cracked and chapped. His mouth was so dry it hurt to open it, and his tongue felt as if it were the size of a beefsteak. Sitting up in the sand, he wiped his eyes on the sleeve of his shirt and stared as a cloud of dust approached him.

What's a stagecoach doing out here?

The bones in his arms and legs ached as he watched the coach toss and sway closer. The cloud of dust swirled over the top of him, and the stage came to a horse-snorting, rig-rattling, leather-creaking, passenger-shouting stop.

Andrews was still sitting in the sand not five feet from a tall, one-limbed saguaro cactus when the door of the stage flew open, and Pepper Paige stepped out. She wore a long-trained, white wedding dress covered with tiny pearls and on her head a white straw hat with a white, lacy ribbon flowing down the back.

"You missed the wedding, Andrews!" she shouted.

"Missed it? But . . . I was tryin' . . . ," he mumbled with a dry mouth. "I . . . eh, I got hurt!"

"Well, that's the last time you're standing me up! You've been late three times to your own wedding. I'm not going through this again!"

"Th-three times?"

"Don't you play dumb with me, Mr. Tapadera Andrews!" She got back into the stage and slammed the door behind her. Then she stuck her head out the window. "I'm going to Tombstone and marry Billy Clanton!"

"Clanton's dead! The Earp brothers shot him down last year!" he called as the stage began to roll.

With her head sticking out the stage window, she shouted back, "Oh, yeah? Well, he's in better shape than you!"

For several minutes he sat and watched the stage roll up the mountain road. A tall plume of dust followed it out of sight.

Someone was grabbing his arm. The sun disappeared. So did the heat. The night was dark. It was cold. It was Colorado.

"Stack?"

Lowery motioned for him to climb off the horse.

The ringing in his ear persisted, and he continued to shout as he struggled to get down off the horse. "Stack? Where are we? I can't hear anything!"

Stack mouthed something, then led Tap toward a small, sagging log cabin no more than eight by ten feet. Leaning Andrews against the door frame, Lowery plunged into the darkness of the cabin. In a matter of minutes, a small fire blazed in the fireplace. Stack mouthed something and signaled for him to come in.

Tap struggled to warm himself in a world of lapping yellow flames and loud ringing noise. Stack packed both saddles and gear into the cabin. He hung a canteen over a hook by the fire and sat down cross-legged on the floor next to Tap.

Leaning over to his left ear, Stack shouted, "That canteen will have to thaw out before you can get a drink!"

"What? Canteen . . . oh, yeah . . . frozen," Tap hollered without hearing himself.

"You took a bad blow to the ear."

"I'm mighty dizzy!"

"You need some sleep."

"Why'd we run out?"

"They was plannin' on shootin' us."

"What?"

"They was—"

"I heard you. What about the girls' money? Are we giving up on findin' it?"

Stack leaned back, dragged his bedroll toward the fire, and untied it. In the middle was a large leather pouch. He tugged it open and dumped the contents onto the blanket. Gold and silver coins tumbled out as well as several pieces of jewelry.

"Is that it?"

Stack nodded his head.

"Where'd you get it?"

Leaning closer, Stack shouted, "While you had Karl diverted, I dug in his saddlebags! Most of the money is still there. That jewelry belongs to April."

"Diversion? Is that what I was doin'?"

"I ain't never seen it done quite that way," Stack admitted. "You were mighty brave to lay down in the middle of the street in the dark."

"I slipped."

"Well, it surely spooked that horse. Don't reckon he's used to hearing voices from off the ground."

"Karl just about beat me to death. Why didn't you help?"

"I was chasing down that spooked horse. Besides, they would have shot me if I had interfered."

"Who?"

"The whole town of Rico Springs. They was bettin' on the fight."

"Who were they bettin' on?"

"Mostly Karl. The old man with the powder burns made a bun-
dle bettin' on you."

"Half-Beard?"

"Is that his name? Once the bets were collected, they wouldn't
have let us leave without a gunfight. Seems like every man you
ever shot has a friend in that crowd."

"Are they goin' to follow us?"

"Not for a while," Stack shouted. "Half-Beard bought the
bunch another round of drinks. Besides, Karl and the others can't
tell them what money we took. The boys there aren't too happy
that April's burnt down."

Tap reached up and took the canteen, swirled it around in his
hands, and gulped down a couple of swallows. "I need some sleep."

Stack was saying something with his face toward the fire.

"What?"

"I said," Stack hollered, "I'm sure glad Pepper girl can't see you
now. She might change her mind. Now go on, get some sleep.
Maybe you'll dream about that yellow-haired girl."

"No!"

"What?" Stack questioned.

"No more dreams!"

There was only a crack of light filtering into the cabin when
Tap opened his eyes. He was lying on his back on the hard-packed
dirt floor of the cabin with his blanket pulled up to his chin. His
hat was mashed beneath his head like a pillow. His bones and
joints ached as he sat up.

The saddles were gone, and he guessed that Stack was outside
rigging up the ponies. He stirred up what was left of the fire and
grabbed the canteen of lukewarm water. After taking a couple
of swigs, he soaked his bandanna and tried cleaning the dried
blood off his knuckles, hands, and face. His right ear felt raw to
the touch.

"Stack?"

*I think I can hear a little better with my left ear! The ringing's
not quite so bad!*

Pounding the crown of his hat back into shape, he gingerly set it on his head and, buttoning his coat, stumbled to the door.

In the morning light, he could see Stack Lowery yank the latigo on his saddle.

"Hey, partner, I think I can hear better!" he called.

"That's mighty good news!"

"What?"

Lowery walked over and shouted at Tap's left ear, "That's mighty good news!"

"Yeah. That's what I'm thinkin'. Maybe this will clear up in a day or two."

"You still feelin' dizzy?"

"What?"

"Dizzy? You still dizzy?"

"Oh, no. I'm okay. You need some help?"

"Nope. I figure if you want to make it to McCurleys' by tonight, we'd best get started."

"McCurleys'?"

"And see Pepper."

"Oh . . . no! Stack, I can't go ridin' in lookin' like this! It might be best if I stay out at the ranch a day or two and then go see her."

"In that case, I say we ride back by April's," Stack hollered.

"What for?"

"Well, the fire will be cooled off, and we can dig around and see if there's anything we can salvage. I'd like to be able to tell April we saved all we could. There might be some jewelry left— you know, silver and gold."

Tap rubbed his hands together and nodded. "It sure is!"

"Sure is what?"

"Shiverin' cold! It's mighty cold." Tap nodded.

It got colder.

Riding east, they took the brunt of the frigid air face-on. The clouds, dark and pregnant, dipped to the ground forming a fog that froze and encased everything in sight. It was what the Shoshones of Nevada called the *pogonip,* and Tap figured it might not be the cause of every infirmity, as the Indians claimed, but it surely aggravated all of his.

By late in the day, they finally reached Pingree Hill. His feet and hands were numb, his ribs ached, his ear throbbed, and his eyelashes had temporarily frozen to his eyebrows. Blinking was impossible.

Using timbers left from the dance hall, they built a huge bonfire across the road from the barn. About an hour after dark a horse trader from Helena rode up to the fire leading a string of five wide-bodied cow ponies. He turned the horses into the corral and joined them at the fire.

Tap watched as the man and Stack visited. Then a farm wagon with four prospectors bound for Arizona came in. After that two drovers from Montana drifted in on broken-down horses. Then a farm tool salesman with a hard-sided wagon joined them around the fire.

Tap could see their disappointment at finding the dance hall gone. He could see their resignation and laughter, their gestures and proclamations. He just couldn't hear anything other than the loud ringing sound and the crackle of the fire. He left to bury his bedroll beneath the large stack of hay in the loft of the barn.

Tap dragged himself out of bed before daybreak, and soon he had the bonfire revived. Every bone in his body ached—but none as severely as the right side of his head. After several cups of boiled coffee, he and Stack sorted through the ruins of the dance hall. Most of the others who had stopped by the night before had slept in the barn also, and all were on their way within the first hour of the day.

Tap wasn't sure what to look for, but he did find several gold and silver lumps that he figured at one time had been coins. However, the high concentration of broken glass made sorting with bare hands dangerous as well as cold.

Stack salvaged several cast-iron pots and skillets from what used to be the kitchen. He found a little purple glass bottle with a glass stopper. The label was burned off.

"Come on, partner," he shouted. "There ain't nothing left here worth savin'!"

"You goin' to take those pans?" Tap called above the ringing noise.

"Nope. They're too heavy. It's time to just walk away. Everything's gone."

"What's in the bottle?"

"It's Rocky's laudanum. Ain't much left, but maybe she'll get some sleep at night."

Mounting their horses, they rode west. Stack pulled up on the first pass and turned in the saddle to look down on Pingree Hill.

"Don't reckon I'll ever be back." He sighed.

Tap didn't hear many of the words, but he could read the meaning in Stack's soft, brown eyes.

It's his whole life, Lord. A woman like April to work for, some girls to take care of. He's a decent man—livin' mostly in an indecent world.

Some parts of the shortcut from Pingree Hill to the Triple Creek Ranch were no more than seven feet wide, and Tap marveled that Stack had managed to bring a wagon load of women through it in the dark. In places grass still showed through the snow. The sky was stuffed with clouds, but it didn't snow. They rode two hours, then stopped to build a fire and rest the horses.

Mounting up, they repeated the process. Stack led the way. Tap rode with his bandanna tied around his face and ears. They didn't slow down at sunset but pressed on through the dark of night. The horses set their own pace for the journey.

About midnight they broke out of the trees on the foothills of the Medicine Bows. They bypassed the house and rode straight to the barn.

It was still icy cold in the room, but Tap had the fire blazing when Stack came in and tossed the saddles down.

"Wiley ain't back yet?" he asked.

"What?"

Stack shouted at Tap's left ear, "Wiley ain't back?"

"Nope," Tap hollered. "No tellin' what the roads are like up in Wyomin'."

"I didn't see any activity at the house. Did you?"

Tap looked Stack in the face. "You figure we ought to go over and check on the women? They might be pretty excited to find out about the money."

Stack sat down on his saddle and tugged at his black stove-top boots. "Let 'em sleep. That little one ain't cryin'; they must be all right. There's smoke in the chimney, so they've got the place warm."

Within two minutes of pulling the dirty wool blankets over his shoulder, Tap fell asleep to the sounds of continuous church bells ringing and two thousand crickets chirping in his right ear.

The air was biting cold, his back was stiff, and the room was pitch-black when Tap blinked his eyes open. He moved his hand across the floor and pulled his Colt .44 from the holster.

Lord, somethin's goin' on. I can sense it, but I can't see it . . . or hear it.

He stood to his feet. A sharp pain shot through his ribs. Barefoot, clutching the gun, he stole to the thin wooden door that separated the tack room from the main part of the barn.

A flicker of light filtered into the barn from the less than air-tight siding. The dirt floor was cold on Tap's feet as he scooted to the main barn door. He threw the latch on the door, swung the door open about eight inches, and peered toward the yard.

Standing not more than a foot in front of the door was a man, his face covered with a dark bandanna, a wide-brimmed hat pushed low. Tap raised and cocked the Colt in one action.

The man jerked the bandanna down immediately. "Whoa! Tap, it's me—Wiley!"

"What?"

"Wiley. It's me—Wiley!" he shouted.

"Oh . . . Wiley! Yeah." Tap shoved the big barn door open and signaled for Wiley to bring his horse inside.

"Didn't you hear me call out?"

Tap shuffled over and lit a lamp. Wiley tugged off his gloves and blew warm air into his hands.

"I said," Wiley began, "why didn't you—good grief! What happened to the side of your head?"

"What? Head? Oh, I ran into a rifle barrel. Can't hear worth beans, Wiley. Would you believe I can't hear anything? Talk to this other ear."

"Did you get April's and the girls' money back?" Wiley hollered.

"Yep. How 'bout you? Get them telegrams sent?"

"Yeah. I also got some news about Fightin' Ed. He's goin' to move you out of here, Tap. He's gone to see some of his friends at the Cheyenne Club."

"Cheyenne? They don't have anything to say about Colorado."

"I hope you're right. . . . How are the girls?"

"What?"

"Girls! How are the girls?"

"We just pulled in a couple hours ago. We let 'em sleep."

"One of 'em ain't sleepin'."

"What?"

"I rode over by there and heard one of 'em cryin'."

"It must be Rocky."

"You and Stack didn't take any lead, did you?"

"Bed? Yeah, go on," Tap urged. "Stack will take care of Rocky."

Wiley started to say something, then shrugged, and put his horse away. Tap woke Stack from a deep sleep. The groggy piano player tugged on his boots and coat and crunched his way across the yard to the house.

Several minutes later he returned carrying a pan covered by a checkered napkin in one hand and the little purple bottle in the other.

"How's she doin', Stack?" Tap called out.

"Better now. That was one happy girl when she saw this." He held up the glass bottle. "They had some extra biscuits in the kitchen."

"Did ya tell 'em about the money?"

"Yep," Stack shouted. "They're so excited they said they was pitchin' us a party tomorrow! Have a biscuit."

Lying on his back on the floor of a fifteen-foot-square, rough wood room filled with saddles, harnesses, bridles, mecates, hackamores, and halters, Tap ate a biscuit and stared into the darkness.

He thought about crying dance-hall girls.

Bank loans.

Fighting Ed.

Outlaws with grudges.

The Arizona Territorial Prison at Yuma.

The wedding.

And Pepper.

Mostly he thought about Pepper.

6

With her sleeves rolled up to her elbows, Pepper stepped to the porch of the Franklin house and mopped the perspiration from her forehead with a flour sack tea towel. The cold December morning felt refreshing on her pale cheeks and face. She had slept little, spending most of the night caring for tiny Rebecca Marie Franklin.

Everything about her is so beautiful, Lord. The little fingers, the nose, the ears, the little, round mouth. Alert brown eyes looking out at a great, big world. Everything's new for her. All the joys, all the sorrows . . . Lord, may there not be many sorrows for her.

Pepper no longer brushed away sweat—but tears—as she stood facing the rising sun over the snowcapped mountains to the east.

I've got to tell Tap about the miscarriage before the wedding, Lord—no matter what. Every day of my life it ties my stomach in knots. The doctor said maybe I couldn't . . . but I know it's just not true! Of course, I can still have children. Cute little ones like Rebecca Marie.

Toting her carefully folded wedding dress to the buggy, Pepper pulled the hood up on her cape, shook hands with a grateful Nat Franklin, and drove north toward McCurleys'. The cold morning air colored her cheeks and numbed her chin, but she kept the tall, gray horse at a comfortable trot.

I'll park in the middle of the yard. Surely Tap will be waiting

*at the hotel. Then he can go out to the corral or something while
I bring the dress into the hotel. He'll pitch a fit, of course, but "the
groom does not get to see the dress, Mr. Tapadera Andrews!" And
he'll give me that hurt little-boy look . . . and I'll . . . I'll probably
kiss him, and he'll slip his strong arms around my waist and I'll
. . . and that's all! He absolutely doesn't get to see it!*

Her mind raced with thoughts of Tap, and the trip passed quickly.
She was surprised to find so many rigs parked around the hotel when
she arrived right before noon. Robert McCurley, vest unbuttoned
and tie hanging crooked, scampered from the barn toward the hotel.

"Pepper, tie that rig off at the barn. I'll be back out in a minute
and put it up. Glad you got back safe. If you're up to it, Mama
could sure use some help. The east pass snowed shut, and most of
the traffic up to Cheyenne is coming through here. A man will
either starve or die of commotion in this business!"

"Did Tap come in from the ranch?"

"Yep."

"Where is he, Mr. Mac? Is he in the house or the barn?"

McCurley stopped and squinted his eyes in his wrinkled, leathery face. "He's gone."

"What do you mean, he's gone?"

"Oh, he came down yesterday. But he didn't stay overnight.
There was trouble up at Pingree Hill. April's place caught fire, and
Stack Lowery asked him to come up and help find the culprits
who did it."

"The dance hall burned? Did anyone get hurt? What about
April? And Danni Mae?"

"Well, I declare . . . I don't know if he told me that or not. It's
just that he and Lowery needed to recover some stolen funds. But
he said not to worry. He'd faced this gang down before."

"What gang?"

"Cain't tell ya that neither." McCurley hustled to the porch.
"But everyone must be fine, or he surely would have told me. He
did say that he'd be gone a few days and then swing down by here
to see you. There's a note fer ya in yer room." McCurley scooted
inside the hotel leaving Pepper sitting in the black buggy.

This isn't the way we planned it! We left Denver saying we would just sit out here—nice and quiet and wait for the wedding.

"Miss Pepper! I'm glad to see you made it back safely!"

A young man in a suit and tie stepped out on the porch. His neatly trimmed sandy hair was parted in the middle.

"Little Bob! I—I, eh, thought you went to Fort Collins."

"Well, wouldn't you know, that pass was snowed shut tighter than a cork stopper on a bottle of champagne."

Pepper drove the black buggy to the barn. Little Bob took the reins from her gloved left hand and tied off the horse while she retrieved her wedding dress.

"Yes, ma'am." He grinned, revealing a full set of clean white teeth. "That snowstorm was, well . . . it was sort of providential, I'd say."

"Providential?"

"You see, I think me—an Easterner just graduated from Yale—meeting you out here in the wilds of Colorado might just be pre-ordained by the Almighty."

Hurrying across the yard full of crusty snow, she stopped to stare at Little Bob. "What does the Lord have to do with you being here?"

"Can't you feel it in your heart of hearts? It sort of tingles way down in your toes and works its way right up to the top of your head. You know what I mean?"

"I haven't the slightest idea what you're talking about, Little Bob. Perhaps you have a chill."

"When I'm around you, Miss Pepper, I feel warm all over!"

She sighed deeply and brushed past him, grasping the wedding dress as he held the door open. She scampered up the polished wooden stairs and into her room with the high ceiling.

Lord, at the dance hall I had to put up with the Little Bobs of the world as long as they paid good money. I'm really, really going to enjoy being a married woman!

For the next several days Pepper helped Mrs. McCurley and her staff cook for the guests. For the most part she succeeded in avoiding Little Bob Gundersen.

Perched on a stool in the kitchen, she sipped a cup of coffee and glanced out the blue gingham curtains toward the yard. On a clear winter day, she could see across the shallow snow- and sage-covered valley for at least thirty miles. The hotel sat like an unwalled fort in a vast expanse of unsettled wilderness.

Is this the way it's going to be? Always waiting for him to return? Always wondering if he's in trouble . . . hurt . . . or . . . dead? He's not a lawman. He's not an outlaw. How does he get mixed up in these things? There's got to be someplace on the face of this earth where we can just sit and watch the world go by— Mama and Daddy on the porch . . . and a passel of kids scamperin' about. Please, Lord, let there be children!

"Excuse me, Miss Pepper, I'm certainly delighted to see I'm not interrupting anything!"

"Oh . . . Little Bob, you startled me. Actually I just finished my coffee. I'm going up to my room and rest a bit before supper. Please help yourself to some coffee. Now if you'll excuse me, I'll—"

"Miss Pepper, it certainly seems like you're avoiding me."

Holding her coffee cup in both hands in front of her, she looked him straight in the eyes. "Of course I am."

"But why?" He glanced down at his slick black leather shoes and rocked back on his heels.

"Little Bob, I'm going to be real honest with you. You are an absolute aggravation. I'm trying to get ready for a wedding to a man I want to spend the rest of my life with, and you're trailing at my heels like a dog with its tongue lolling out. This is really getting on my nerves, and I want it to stop. Do you understand what I'm saying?"

"Yes, ma'am." He grinned from ear to scrubbed-clean ear. "I feel the same way."

"You do?"

"Sure. It's sort of a tingly feeling in the nerves, isn't it? Starts down at your toes and then—"

"You didn't even hear a word I said! This is incredible! Little Bob, what did they teach you at Yale anyway?"

"Dams."

"What?"

"I graduated in engineering. Dams, aqueducts, canals—that sort of thing. Do you know that one day this whole West will be irrigated farmland?"

"What I mean is, didn't they teach you not to badger ladies?"

"Yes, ma'am. And anytime you find me even mildly vexatious, you just say so, and I'll leave."

"So!" She scowled.

"Huh?"

Throwing up her hands, she sighed. "Never mind. I really need to go upstairs. Don't you have somewhere to go? Like maybe—home?"

"Oh, no. My parents think a stay in the West will be good for me. Besides, they're in Europe for Christmas this year. My mother's from Austria, you know."

"Eh, no. I didn't know that, Little Bob."

"Yes, in fact I have a cousin who is probably going to marry the duke's son. But you don't have to call me Little Bob. My friends in the East call me Robert."

"Good day, Little Bob." She put her empty coffee cup on the light green wooden counter and brushed past him into the dining room where the table was being set for the next meal.

Why do they come west? They don't work. They don't contribute anything. They don't build. They just watch from the rail. Go home, Little Bob! Go to California. Go build a dam. Go to Austria. Go to Australia, wherever that is!

By taking her meals in the kitchen, bypassing the parlor, and spending most of the day in her room, she avoided not only Little Bob, but most of the other guests at the hotel as well.

After supper on Thursday Bob McCurley burst through the swinging doors into the kitchen, chewing on an unlit cigar.

"Pepper girl, the guests in the parlor are complaining about not getting to visit enough with the yellow-haired beauty. Do you suppose you could break away and accommodate them with some conversation?"

"You mean, Little Bob Gundersen is asking for me?"

"Actually it was some others that mentioned it. There's a hard-

ware man who just came down from Pingree Hill. He might have
some news on April and the others."

"You got to promise that if Little Bob gets me cornered, you'll
come pull me out."

"I promise. Thanks, Pepper. I ain't never known a woman who
could visit with so many men at once like you."

*That's because you've never spent much time in the hurdy-
gurdys and dance halls!*

She brushed her blonde hair back with her fingers and reset the
pearl combs. Then she rolled down the sleeves of her beaded yellow dress, buttoned them, and brushed her skirt. With a pattern
she had used for years, she smiled and promenaded into the parlor.

Within three minutes Pepper was surrounded by a half-dozen
men who seemed to be all talking to her at once. The subjects
ranged from the latest fashions in New Orleans to reports of a
new gold strike in the San Juan Mountains.

"Did you say you just came down from Pingree Hill?" she
asked the short, bald man with a full beard.

"Yes, Miss Pepper, and I might add it was a disappointment to
see the dance hall burned down—not that I'm the type of man
normally to stop at such a place, mind you, but I had hoped for a
spot of, er, refreshment."

"You mean, there's no one left living there at all?"

"Well, the barn and the corrals are still standing and the privies, but that's it. I didn't see a soul anywhere."

"Where did Mrs. Hastings and the others go?"

"Hastings?"

"April Hastings—the proprietress. Did they go to Fort
Collins?"

A middle-aged man with distinguished flecks of gray at his tem-
ples and small, gold wire-framed eyeglasses spoke up. "I heard
someone say that they all moved to Laramie City."

"Laramie City? That's, eh, a long way."

*Danni Mae will miss the wedding! She promised to sing and . . .
and Stack needs to be there!*

"Say, Miss Pepper." She turned to see Thom Moran stroll over
with his brown vest buttoned too tight and his hands jammed into

his back pockets. "When's the weddin'? Ain't that coming up any day now?"

"It's just a week away, Thom. Thanks for asking."

"I almost stopped in to see old Tap myself. I was up that way yesterday doing a little hunting."

"Oh, I don't think he's at the ranch now."

"Well, by golly, someone's there. I was clean over in the Independence Hills, but I could see a column of smoke from the ranch house. 'Yes, sir,' I said to myself, 'Tap's in there warmin' by the fire.'"

"Oh, it might be Wiley. He's got a man named Wiley helping at the ranch."

"The Wiley who used to work at the Rafter R?" a man with dark circles under his eyes and a drooping mustache asked.

"Yes. Do you know him?"

"I ran across him two days ago up on the Wyomin' border. He said he was on his way to Laramie City to send a couple telegrams."

If Wiley's not at the ranch, who's burning a fire in the house?

The talk soon turned to a debate over whether Missouri's Governor Crittenden should have granted a pardon to Bob Ford after Ford shot Jesse James in the back. The division of opinion seemed to be split at the Mason-Dixon line, and Pepper excused herself before talk turned to the war of rebellion—or of secession—depending on the loyalties of the speaker.

She pushed her way into the kitchen to say good night to Mrs. McCurley and stumbled into Little Bob barging into the parlor. Although she had not lost her footing, he reached out and held her shoulders.

"Are you all right, Miss Pepper?"

"Little Bob, would you please take your hands off my shoulders."

"Yes, ma'am. I was just trying to—"

"I know exactly what you were trying to do."

"Boy, I'm glad I ran into you."

"Obviously." She glared. "Now remove your hands!"

"No, what I mean is . . ." He let his hands drop to his side, but he took a step closer, standing only a few inches from her. "I wanted to talk to you about our conversation the other day. You know, you were absolutely correct in what you said."

Stepping back an arm's length from him, she tilted her head to the right. "Well, I'm glad you see it my way. It shows real maturity, Little Bob."

"Yes, I know. You said that it was best in the long run to be real honest with each other. And I've been thinking for two days, that's exactly my problem. I just haven't had the nerve to speak up and be honest. So here goes. I'm sure everyone can tell that I'm madly in love with you. So that's no secret. But to be real honest, I want you to know that I plan on making you my wife and have you move with me back to Baltimore."

With her hands on her hips, Pepper stared in disbelief. "You've got to be kidding!"

"No, ma'am. I promised to tell you the truth, and that's the gospel truth."

"Look, Little Bob, get something into your head. In a few days I'm going to marry Tap Andrews—a man I love and want to spend my life with." Her throat was tense as each word darted from her lips. "You are no longer merely annoying, but you are getting close to abusing this relationship. Perhaps you're not aware of how such offenders are dealt with in the West. Mr. Andrews packs a Winchester '73 and a Colt .44. He has spent his life pointing it at men and pulling the trigger. I, too, often carry a .32 Colt and, if necessary, will not hesitate to use it, as I have had to do on several occasions. This is Colorado, not Connecticut. Your advances will not be tolerated any longer!"

Little Bob stood next to her, scratching the back of his head with his mouth gaping open. "I, eh, I . . . don't know what to say. So I am starting to get to you? Is that what you said?"

"What I said was that if you continue to harass me or reach out and grab me as you did when I entered this room, either I or the man I'm about to marry will shoot you."

The smile dropped off his face.

"That's what I love about this country. Folks aren't afraid to relax and tease each other. Back east most people would have taken that seriously. Yes, ma'am, they would have."

Pepper stared at Little Bob Gundersen.

There is no way possible you could ever have graduated from college!

She marched out of the kitchen and straight to her room. For the first time since moving in, she locked the door. Bob McCurley had a fire burning in the white fireplace. After hanging her dress in the wardrobe, she scooted the green Queen Anne chair over to the hearth and plopped down.

Lord, I don't know why I get so mad at Little Bob. I'm glad I have this room to come to. This has been the only place in my whole life where I've felt perfectly safe. I want a whole house that's just mine—I mean, mine and Tap's. A house where there aren't drunks downstairs or Little Bobs in the parlor.

I need some rest.

I need to see Tap.

He must be at the ranch if Wiley's in Laramie city. He might be hurt. He might need somebody there to doctor him.

Sometime within the next half hour Pepper Paige, wearing petticoats, fell asleep in the chair in front of the fire, but not before deciding to go to the ranch and check on Tap.

Bob McCurley had the buggy hitched up and waiting out front before Pepper finished eating breakfast at the big butcher's block in the center of the kitchen.

"Mrs. Mac, please don't tell Little Bob what direction I went. I'm getting so tired of him pestering me."

"I thought for sure he'd go back east for Christmas," the gray-headed woman said.

"He told me he was going to stay in the West, but I don't know how long his money will last." Pepper fastened the top pearl button on her high-necked chocolate brown dress and pulled on her coat and her hooded cape.

"Some of 'em never seem to run out of money. Sort of makes you think their kin wants 'em not to come home. I think Little Bob went out huntin' early. I haven't seen him all mornin'."

"Listen, if Tap's not feelin' well, I might spend the night, but he's got a friend out there, and I promise it will be proper."

"Now look at you—you talkin' to me as if I was your mama."

"Well, aren't you?" Pepper teased.

"Go on, girl. Go take care of Mr. Andrews. Enjoy it. In another seven days you won't have any other choice."

Pepper slipped past the pots and pans hung from the pounded copper ceiling and into the yard. A couple of men were awkwardly trying to rope horses in the corrals. Climbing into the buggy, she tugged the thick buffalo robe over her legs and was glad that Mr. McCurley hadn't put any coals in the warming box.

It was a long ride but a familiar one. Pepper's mind flitted from weddings . . . to babies . . . to Tap . . . to bank loans due . . . to burned-down dance halls . . . to working at dance halls . . . and back to Tap.

She had just crossed the frozen river when she caught sight of a rider following along several miles behind. As she started the ascent up into Triple Creek Valley, she thought she saw the rider once more.

I can't believe this! Surely Little Bob wouldn't do this to me after that scolding I gave him yesterday!

She drove the buggy up to the second grove of juniper trees, tied it off, and threw her cape over a small tree near the rear of the buggy. Carrying her satchel, she hiked back to the first cluster of trees and waited.

Pepper shivered as a rider approached. Hiding behind the cover of the trees, she watched Little Bob ride past her and slowly approach the buggy. Pepper crept up behind him and pulled her .32 sheathed-triggered "Lady Colt" out of the satchel.

Little Bob stopped about twenty feet from the buggy and hollered from the saddle toward the caped evergreen. "Miss Pepper? Are you feeling all right?"

The sound of her .32 cocking caused him to spin around in the saddle and fumble clumsily at his rifle scabbard.

"Miss Pepper! You startled me. I thought—I thought you . . . Is that just your cape up there?"

"Little Bob, my range with this revolver is about fifty feet. I do not want you within fifty feet of me for the rest of my life. Do you understand?"

"Miss Pepper, don't go pointing that gun. This isn't a very funny game."

"It's not a game, Little Bob. Why are you following me?"

"Oh, no, I assure you. I was out hunting. I wanted to try out this new Sharps 'Creedmoor.'" He pointed at the scabbard. "But it just happened that I cut across your trail and wanted to make sure you got safely to wherever it is you're going. You're headed for that ranch, aren't you?"

"Please leave now!" she demanded, raising the gun and aiming at his chest.

"Did you ever notice how agitated you get when I'm around? I had this class in behaviorism, and they said that such actions meant that you are secretly attracted to me. This might come as a surprise, but in the East many women seemed fairly indifferent to me."

"At the count of three, Little Bob, I'm pulling this trigger."

"You know, Miss Pepper, I've been out west for almost four months, and you're the first person to threaten to shoot me."

"I find that hard to believe."

"The way they talked back at school you'd think everyone west of Kansas was a bloodthirsty killer. But don't worry about me. I'll just lag along behind you to see that you make it to the ranch and . . ."

Pointing the gutta-percha-handled .32 rimfire to a spot in the frozen roadway about five feet to the left of Bob's horse's front feet, she squeezed the trigger. The noise of the gunfire coupled with the bits of frozen roadway spraying up on the horse caused the animal to turn and bolt at a full gallop toward the southwest. Even as the gun recoiled in her hand, Pepper could see Little Bob struggling to keep on the horse and bring it under control.

Pepper hiked back to the buggy, retrieved her cape, and once again set out for the ranch.

I know, I know, I should be more patient. Lord, teach me to be a gracious married lady. I know Little Bob will not be the last jerk I have to deal with.

Even though the clouds hung heavy and low, bringing a damp coldness, Pepper felt flushed with anger and some remorse as she drove on. Any trace of the sun was completely buried by the impending storm, yet she sensed that it was a little past noon.

The smoke from the house and the woodstove in the barn both rose straight up and seemed to be held suspended like two ancient, crumbling marble columns.

He is home! Probably was going to wait until tomorrow to come to McCurleys'. Maybe he's fixing something to eat. I wonder if that Mr. Wiley's around? I hope not. Well, Lord, what I mean is—I hope Tap and I have some time when we can . . . talk private-like and . . . well, You know what I mean.

She drove to the west of the leafless cottonwoods and parked behind the woodshed and the tiny blacksmith shop. Pepper was startled to hear voices coming from inside the house.

That can't be a woman's voice! Who's here?

As she slipped up to the front door, she glanced around the yard looking for signs of another buggy or carriage.

This is strange. Is that banker back? Or maybe . . .

She heard a woman laugh and call out something about a dance. She paused, her gloved hand in the air, and then rapped the door with several hard knocks.

"Tap, it's my turn to . . ." A girl with big, hollow eyes and straight, dark hair stopped giggling when she saw Pepper. She wore an oversized dance-hall dress that would have been revealing if there had been anything to reveal.

"Who are you?" Pepper demanded.

"Well, who are *you?*" the girl asked.

Pepper could feel the anger burn in her throat. "I demand to know who you are!" she shouted.

"I don't think I like you!" the girl retorted and then slammed the door.

What is this?

Pepper banged repeatedly on the door.

This time a woman with long black hair hanging to her waist and olive-colored skin opened the door.

"Selena?" Pepper choked.

"Well, well, well. The yellow-haired dance-hall queen has come to visit us!"

"Us? What do you mean us?"

"Now you didn't really think you could keep that cowboy happy all by yourself, did you?" Selena purred.

Pepper stormed through the rough wooden doorway. "What in the world is going . . ."

Danni Mae ran out of the kitchen wearing a soiled apron over her dress and smelling of baked bread.

"Pepper! Honey, what a wonderful surprise! Tap didn't say anything about you coming to visit today!" Danni Mae threw her arms around Pepper and squeezed hard. "I guess you heard about April's?"

"What's going on here, Danni Mae?" She turned to see another woman step forward. "Paula?"

"Pepper! Hi! Your Tap is quite some guy."

"Oh?"

"He and Stack went out and got our money back from those outlaws."

"But what are you doing here?"

"Oh," Selena broke in, "so the *vaquero* just happened to forget to tell you that he invited us girls to stay with him until after the wedding?"

"He did what?"

Danni Mae grabbed Pepper's hand and led her into the hot, steamy kitchen. "Listen, girl, we were freezing, scared, and had no place to go, so Stack bundled us into the wagon and drove us out here. We are on our way to Wyoming, but Tap was afraid we wouldn't be back for the weddin', so he invited us to stay at the ranch."

The girl who first met her at the door scooted into the kitchen.

"Danni Mae," she twittered, "can you tie this ribbon straight for me? When it's behind my head, I always get it crooked."

Swirling around, turning her back toward Danni Mae, she looked Pepper in the eyes. "I don't think I'm goin' to like you," she informed Pepper.

Pepper was still staring with her mouth open when the girl ran back out to the front room.

"Who is that?"

"Rocky. She's a new girl at the dance hall."

"How old is she?"

"Says she's eighteen. I figure it's more like sixteen."

"If that. What's she doing working at April's?"

"How old were you when you started letting those drunks and deadbeats in Boise City twirl you around the dance hall?"

"Eh . . . fifteen, but I—"

"Yeah, me too. Don't mind her. She gets real cranky when she doesn't have her medicine." Danni Mae raised her eyebrows.

"Laudanum or opium?" Pepper asked.

"Laudanum. It shows, doesn't it?"

The two walked back out to the front room and stopped near the piano. "Danni Mae, where's Tap?"

"In the barn, I suppose. We were tryin' to get things ready for the party."

"What party?"

"We wanted to thank the men for recoverin' our poke," Paula explained.

"Men? Oh, is Stack here, too?"

"Sure." Danni Mae grinned. "He'll be tickled to see you. And then there's Wiley. He's a nice man."

Pepper caught a lilt in Danni Mae's voice. "How nice?"

"Really, really nice." Danni Mae winked.

"That's what I thought." Pepper scowled. "Now just exactly how do all seven of you fit in this house?"

"Oh, the men sleep out in the tack room."

"And," Selena cooed, "we have to sleep in Señor Andrews's bed. We're sort of breakin' it in for you, honey!"

"Don't pay her no mind," Danni Mae advised. "All of us girls are camped in that room. Except for Rocky. She's in the attic."

"This place has an—an attic?" Pepper stammered.

"Oh, that Tapadera is just full of surprises, isn't he, *mi alma?*" Selena wrapped her long hair around and covered her face like a veil.

"I'm going out to the barn," Pepper announced.

"You cain't," Rocky hollered from near the fireplace. "The barn is off limits to us women. That's what Tap said. He won't let none of us go out there no matter how lonesome we get."

"I can assure you, it is not off limits to me!" Pepper raged out the door leaving it wide open.

Getting the bed ready! Tap, how could you do this to me? Didn't you know how Selena would use this? I can't believe you'd actually invite her to stay for the wedding!

Pepper tugged open the big wooden door and barged into the cavernous barn. With the daylight behind her, she waited for her eyes to adjust to the dimness. She turned toward a banging sound and spotted Tap nailing a horseshoe on Brownie's right rear hoof.

"Tap, I can't believe for one minute that you'd let Selena move into our . . . your bedroom . . . eh, house! You know perfectly well how I feel about her!"

He continued shoeing the horse, refusing to look toward her or even acknowledge her presence.

"Tap, are you listening to me? We haven't seen each other for days, and you're going to pretend like I'm not even here? I want to know right now why you didn't ask me about Selena and the girls staying at the ranch!"

He reached to his mouth and grabbed another horseshoe nail and began driving it through the shoe into the hoof. She thought she heard him humming a tune.

"You think this is funny? You think this is a little game? You think you can play around with my emotions? Well, I can tell you one thing, Mr. Tapadera Andrews, I have half a mind to call off the whole wedding! You can't treat me this way, Tap. Tap! Are you going to say something or not?" she shouted.

"Pepper, girl, what's all the screaming?"

Stack Lowery stepped out of the tack room. His shirt was unbuttoned and untucked, revealing the strength of his chest.

"Stack! I've been talking to this man for five minutes, and he won't even turn around and say a word. You tell him that I'm going back to McCurleys', and I don't care if I ever—"

"Pepper, you're lookin' mighty fine! And don't pay Tap no mind. He can't hear you."

"Can't hear?"

"Didn't you see that ear? He busted it. He doesn't hear anything but a shout into his left ear."

"He what? How—but . . ."

"He took a hard blow from a rifle barrel. His left ear seems to be gettin' better unless there's a lot of other noises. Here, I'll get him."

"But I . . . He didn't hear?"

Lowery walked over and poked Tap in the shoulder.

"You got company, partner!" he shouted.

"What?"

"Compadre!" Stack hollered. "There's a mighty purdy yellow-haired girl here to see you!"

Tap whipped around.

"Pepper!" He yanked the nails from his mouth and tossed down the hammer.

"Tap, your ear. It's all swollen, and your face is black and blue! Honey, you look awful!"

"What?"

Pepper ran to Tap and threw her arms around him. "You look horrible!" she cried out in his left ear.

"Yeah. Isn't that a mess? But we got the girls' money!" He held her tight.

Real tight.

It was the best Pepper had felt in a week.

"Does it hurt?" she asked loudly.

"As long as I keep busy, it's all right. Can't sleep good though. Stack's snorin' keeps me awake."

"Snoring? I thought you couldn't hear."

"I can't. Now you know how loud he snores." He grinned. "What are you doin' here? I wanted to heal up a little before you had to look at me. Boy, am I glad you came out. We've surely got a lot to talk about!"

She pushed away a little bit but remained in his arms. "What about the bank loan?"

"What about that Franklin baby?" he asked.

"Baby's fine," she shouted.

"I've got Wade checkin' into the loan!" He looked her over again. "You've got to be just about the prettiest thing in the world."

"What do you mean 'just about'?"

"Oh—you *are* the prettiest."

She thought she saw a twinkle in his tired, hurting eyes.

"Guess what? Danni Mae and all the girls are over at the house. They didn't have a place to stay, and I knew you were plannin' on havin' them at the wedding . . . so I just invited the whole bunch. I knew that's what you'd want." He grinned.

She didn't.

7

Sitting in the hayloft, Pepper scooted closer to Tap, holding his left arm with both hands and leaning toward his face. Even on a December afternoon the hay smelled fresh and slightly warm.

"Are you gettin' cold, darlin'?" he asked, slipping his arm around her shoulder and squeezing her close. Although they were in the shadows, he still noticed a sparkle in her green eyes.

She shook her head, then laughed.

"What's the matter?" he asked.

"Look at us." She spoke loudly enough for Tap to hear. "This is our ranch, our dream house, the place where we hide from our pasts and live the quiet life. It's supposed to be our little island of peace and serenity. I've been in dance halls that were quieter than that house!"

He laughed with her. "How can a place so remote be so crowded? What a pair to draw to . . . Everywhere we go people start driftin' in. Do you think it's always goin' to be this way?"

"I surely hope not, but it's all right—this week." Tap's arm felt good on her shoulder. Safe. Warm. Loving.

Tap pushed his hat back and gently brushed his right ear.

"Does it hurt bad?"

"Mainly just itches, but it surely does ring loud. Don't know if I'll ever hear much out of that ear again. No need to fret about that. It feels a whole lot better than a bullet." He squeezed her hand. "Well, Miss Pepper . . . here we are, hiding in the loft like a couple of school kids just to get a little privacy. Yes, ma'am, stick with me, and I'll show you a mighty fine time!"

"You promise?" she murmured.

"What?"

"A good time! You heard me, Andrews!" She punched him in the arm, and he rolled back in the loose hay. "I can see it now," she hollered. "Anytime you want to ignore me, you'll just pretend you didn't hear."

"Do you aim on tellin' me somethin' I don't want to hear?"

"I just might!" she called, rolling over, straddling his stomach, and pinning his arms down. His tired, brown eyes stared up out of an unshaven face.

"It's goin' to be a long wait 'til Friday," he said softly.

"It's been a long two months!" She sighed, releasing the grip on his wrists.

"Huh?"

"I said, 'It's been a long two months!'" she shouted.

"Hey, what's goin' on up there?" a woman called out from the barn floor.

Pepper stood up quickly, brushed the straw out of her dress, and peeked over the edge of the loft.

"Oh, hi, Danni Mae. We were . . . discussing the . . . you know, wedding."

"Sounds to me like you were discussin' the honeymoon! Listen, you two, dinner is finally ready. It's time for the party to begin."

"We'll be over in a minute. Do you want us to call Wiley and Stack?"

"Everyone is already over at the house."

"They are?"

"They have been for half an hour."

"Go ahead and start without us," Pepper called. "We got some more . . . talking to do."

"Okay, we'll start without you. But if you don't show up soon, I'll send Selena over to roust you out."

"Don't you dare!"

Danni Mae waved and walked toward the barn door. "I don't think I've ever seen you so happy. You two be good, you hear?"

Pepper stuck her tongue out at Danni Mae, then smiled, and waved.

"What did Danni Mae want?" Tap called.

"Couldn't you hear?"

"Nope."

"Oh, she just said the others were going to get the party started without us."

"That's all?"

"More or less. I told her we were discussing the wedding," she hollered.

He reached up and took her hand and then pulled her down to the hay where he was still sprawled.

"What about those wedding plans? Have you changed it all around again?" he chided.

"No," she insisted. "'Course I'll have to get the reverend's approval."

"When's he gettin' out to the ranch?"

"He said he'll plan on being here by midmorning."

"Where's he spending the night?"

"At McCurleys'. I've got him registered to have my room. I won't be needing it, you know."

"Say that a little louder, would you?" he prodded.

"What I said was," she shouted, "that you and me are going to be in the big bed in that big house all by ourselves on our wedding night!" She scooped up a flake of hay and tossed it at him.

Dodging the hay, Tap rolled to his feet and stepped around to the front of the loft. He swung out the big wooden door that opened out to the hoist. Standing in the cold breeze, he looked out across the yard at the ranch house. Even though it was only midafternoon, the lanterns were lit and casting a dim light out into the darkly clouded day. There was a frigid smell of snow in the air, but none had fallen for over a week.

Staying out of the cold breeze, Pepper plopped down in the hay next to the door. "What are you looking at, cowboy?" she called out.

He tilted his head, and she repeated the question.

"Oh . . . just thinkin' how much I like this place. It's sort of all the same color at this time of the year, but the land is so quiet—so peaceful. Any direction you turn, it's mighty tranquil—even if the house is full of folks. Out in those hills," he pointed to the west, "there is not a single soul for a hundred miles! Same is true to the east. Up north is the state line, and to the south—only McCurleys'. Sometimes I feel like Abraham reaching Canaan land."

"It won't always be this wide open," she called.

Tap walked to the edge of the opening and leaned against the door frame. The air felt refreshing to his sore ear. Suddenly a little chip of wood flew off the rough wood door casing about two feet above and to the right of his head.

He leaned out to examine what made the wood fly off, and another place about the size of a nickel shattered into splinters only a feet away from his hand.

"Tap!" Pepper screamed and tackled him back into the hayloft. "Someone's shooting at you!"

"What?"

"Didn't you hear that gunshot? Someone's shootin' at you!"

He rolled to his left, drew his Colt, and peered out through a crack in the barn wall.

Lord, I can't keep us alive if I can't hear gunshots!

"Where'd the shots come from?" he hollered.

"They were long-distance shots," she called. "Maybe out in those hills."

"How many shots?"

"Two or three . . . I don't know!"

"Come on! I want you in the house!" Tap grabbed her arm and tugged her toward the ladder. When they reached the front of the barn, they saw Wiley and Stack standing on the front porch aiming carbines toward the west. He and Pepper sprinted to the porch, Tap still carrying his Colt in his right hand.

"What are they shootin' at?" Stack yelled at him.

"Me." Tap shoved Pepper inside the house and then joined the two men. "How many shots you hear?" he asked.

"Three," Wiley replied. "He's a long ways away."

"Two of the shots came fairly close. He must have been sightin' it in. I think I'll saddle Brownie and go take a look," Tap decided.

"Don't you figure that's just what the old boy is hopin' for?"

Stack questioned.

"I don't aim to ride straight at him. Thought I'd drop behind the barn, swing into the trees on the north, and circle back."

"We'll ride with you. You can't hear a thing, and you'll be makin' noise you don't even hear," Wiley offered.

"What?"

"He said we're ridin' with you!" Stack shouted.

"Nope. It's my ranch. Besides, you'll need to stay here to watch over the ladies."

"Wiley can do that."

"And who's goin' to watch over Wiley? I can be real quiet if I don't have you two to shout at. I better go tell Pepper."

Stack stood guard as Tap and Wiley entered the house. The table was piled with steaming food, and the girls were scrubbed clean, doing their best to make their only dresses look fancy.

Rocky had put her dark hair neatly up in combs. Her green dress was trimmed with a white sash about her extremely thin waist. Her eyes were slightly glazed as she threw her arms around Tap's neck and sighed. "Do you want to dance with me, cowboy? I hear there's lots of room out in the barn."

Shaking his head, Tap stammered, "Wh-what?"

Pepper sailed over and tugged Tap away. "He's a lousy dancer," she explained.

"I don't like her!" Rocky complained to Tap. "She's too pushy! Too pushy and too pretty!"

"Eh . . . listen," Tap quickly intervened with Pepper still on his arm. His voice was embarrassingly loud and almost at a monotone. "You all go ahead with the party. I'm goin' to circle around and see if I can figure out who was target-practicin' on the barn. I'll be back in a few minutes."

Pepper walked out to the porch with him.

"See or hear anything, Stack?" he asked.

"Nope," Stack shouted. "You ever have problems with Indians down here?"

"Not yet. Go on in. The party's about to begin."

"You think someone ought to stand guard?"

"Stand guard? Anyone who will fire from that distance isn't

interested in coming right into the yard. Go on in. But keep that Colt strapped to your waist!" Tap hollered.

Stack tipped his hat and scooted inside.

"Tap, it may be a man named Bob Gundersen who's taking shots at you."

"Who?"

She moved very close to his left ear. "Little Bob Gundersen . . . at McCurleys'. Did you ever meet him?"

Tap strained to hear each word. "The university fellow from back east?"

"Yes."

"Why would he want to shoot at me?"

"Eh . . . he's a . . . Well, I wasn't going to tell you, but he's been a real pest, following me around and everything."

"Everything?"

"Well, you know, it's sort of like an infatuation. He thinks . . . you know," she mumbled, "that he's in love with me and I should marry him."

"What? What did you say?"

"Never mind. I think he's jealous of you, and he followed me out here from McCurleys'."

"All the way to the ranch?"

"Almost. I had to chase him off with a gun."

"You what? Was he trying to be forward with you?"

"Not exactly. He's just like a dog that you have to chase away every once in a while. But he did talk about some fancy new rifle he was testing."

"Rifle? Did you say rifle? What kind of rifle?"

"A Sharps something or other."

"Sharps? That could do it from that distance!"

"Well, be careful. I've got to figure out how to keep you out of gunfights for a few more days."

"Oh, there won't be any fightin'. Whoever done it will be long gone. I just want to check out the tracks and see if I can figure out who it was. I'll be back, and we'll have a nice little party. Maybe Stack will play some real dancin' music."

"If he does, I'm locking that Rocky in the attic," Pepper proclaimed.

"She surely does crave affection," Tap added.

"I think she's craving more than just affection."

"You think she's kind of gone over the hill?"

"She wouldn't be the first young dance-hall girl to do so."

"Well, you certainly have my permission to keep her away from me."

"Mr. Tapadera Andrews, I don't need your permission to keep her and all the rest away from you! You're stuck with me, remember?"

"What did you say?"

Pepper detected a sly grin. She stood on her tiptoes and planted a soft kiss on his dry, chapped lips. When she pulled back, he started to say something, but Pepper seemed to anticipate the words, shook her head no, and waved to him as she slipped back into the ranch house.

The ringing in his ear gave every action the same musical background. Tap rode Brownie into the piñon pines and junipers just to the east of the corrals. Then he circled north through a clump of leafless aspens and down a draw to the west that crossed the creek but kept him hidden from the ranch house and the hills where the shots came from.

Tap pulled his '73 Winchester out of the scabbard and laid it across his lap. His dirty canvas coat was pushed back behind his holster. He kept his ungloved right hand in his coat pocket.

Staring out from a six-day beard, he surveyed the rolling, sage-dotted hills ahead of him. The lack of cover and the thin crust of snow insured visibility of the tracks. But it also meant he had no place to hide.

His hands, feet, and face turned numb after an hour of searching. He found no tracks to the north or west.

Cutting a wide circle to the south, Tap came across two sets of hoofprints about five miles from the house.

He rubbed the horse's neck. "Well, Brownie, this old boy rode up toward the house and then turned around and headed south. Looks like he might be slantin' toward McCurleys'."

Maybe Pepper's right about Little Bob, but then I'm not even sure this is the one who took shots at the barn.

Following the tracks back toward the ranch, he came to a snow-covered rocky knoll at least half a mile from the barn. His '73 in hand, Tap slid from the saddle and stalked over to the rocks. The snow revealed imprints of earlier activity.

He kept the horse in that wallow, laid in those rocks, rested the rifle on that boulder, fired it, and then picked up his brass.

Tap scrunched down in the snow, lying exactly in the man's imprint. Holding his Winchester, he took careful aim on the big barn door over twelve hundred yards away.

If he knew his gun, if he had long-range sights, he could surely hit the barn door . . . with any luck. If he had a Sharps, he could have killed me! But that university man didn't seem like the type to be real proficient at long range. Maybe a buffalo hunter . . . but not a kid out of college trying out a new gun.

Tap cocked the .44-40, flipped up the sights, set his finger on the trigger, and listened to the ringing in his ear.

But why would a university man pick up the brass? Some rich guy out west on a lark . . . but who knows? Maybe there is some brass in this snow. It's not nearly as crusty in the shade of these rocks.

Andrews raised the vertical adjustment on the upper tang peep sight, then pulled off his left glove and raised his hand, trying to sense the wind. He pinched the horizontal eye cup a little to the right. Then, taking aim in the middle of the barn loft door, which was no larger than the peep sight hole, he squeezed the trigger.

That ought to get their attention in the house. But it doesn't look like anyone's coming to the porch. Maybe with this drift, forty grains of powder isn't enough bang to be heard in the house.

The blast reverberated in his right ear and sent vibrations down the side of his face that either tingled with extreme pain or extreme pleasure—he couldn't tell which. Tap cocked the lever, ejecting the brass, and pumped a new cartridge into the chamber. Still lying in the rocks, he reached over to retrieve the casing and then jerked his hand back.

There it is! That's where he dropped the brass.

Tap studied the imprint where an earlier brass casing had fallen to the snow.

A half inch longer but only a little fatter. That isn't a .50 . . . probably a .45! A .45 with a lot of powder behind it—maybe a .45-60 or even a .45-75! This old boy's got a '76 Winchester. No wonder he had to lay it on the rocks. No wonder he could blast the barn from here! It shouldn't be too tough to follow those tracks lookin' for a '76. Yet Pepper said Little Bob had a Sharps. 'Course maybe he doesn't know what he has.

Tap studied the west as the sun set on the continental divide. Then he gazed back at the column of smoke drifting up from the ranch house.

"Just an hour, Brownie. We'll follow him for an hour more. There's a pretty yellow-haired girl at a party down there, and I don't aim to make her wait up half the night."

For the first time in two days he could hear himself talk, just a little, in his right ear.

The first miles of the trail were easy to follow. But when Andrews hit the frozen creek, it was not obvious whether the rider had turned north or south. Whichever direction, he seemed to have ridden his horse on top of the ice. Tap followed the slippery creek south for a while, but the shadows of twilight and absence of signs on the icy surface caused him to rein up and turn back toward the ranch.

I can check out Little Bob when I take Pepper back to McCurleys' . . . tomorrow! But it's got me wonderin'. A man who's a pretty fair shot with a big bore, picks up his brass, covers his track by riding down the frozen creek bed. That doesn't really sound like a tenderfoot from Connecticut.

Pepper grabbed his arm the minute he walked through the front door. After giving them all a description of the sniper's lair he had discovered in the rocks, Tap scooted up to the table and filled himself with boiled potatoes, beef chops, gravy, sourdough biscuits, and strawberry preserves.

With Pepper still on his arm, he sat at the table sipping coffee and listening as Stack and Danni Mae entertained with song after song. The music and the words competed for his attention. He could understand very little.

"I wish I could hear them a little better," he called out to Pepper. "Must be funny. Everyone's laughing."

"Or bawdy. Danni Mae mainly knows saloon tunes!"

"What?"

"Forget it. Come on, cowboy, let's go for a walk."

"Go for a talk?"

"Yeah, that'll do."

She led him toward the front door.

"Well, where do you two think you're goin'?" Selena called out.

"We're going to the barn—to check on the horses," Pepper replied. "And the first one who comes out the door after us, I will personally horsewhip!"

Pepper laid her head on Tap's shoulder and held on to his canvas coat sleeve as they walked to the barn. She could hear their feet crunch in the crusted snow—and knew that Tap couldn't. He lit a lantern in the barn and another in the tack room. Then he began to build a fire in the little black potbellied stove.

She dragged a short, heavy bench made from a split log close to the stove and sat down on one end. With the fire blazing, Tap pulled a blanket out of his bedroll and stacked it on her lap.

"It gets cold out here even with a fire," he explained.

"I'm fine . . . the cool air feels good. The hotel's been so hot lately. I've been miserable." Pepper spoke loudly, but didn't shout.

"Yeah. Me, too. . . . It seems like I've been cold ever since we came back from Denver."

"No," she corrected. "I said I was warm."

He tilted his head sideways. "Yeah, but no matter how long the winter, spring is comin'."

"Actually, what I meant was . . . Oh, never mind. You look tired."

"Tired? Yeah. It's like every bone in my body is wantin' some rest."

She patted the folded blanket in her lap. "Why don't you take a nap?"

"A nap?" he called out.

Pepper nodded her head and patted the blanket again.

Tap hung his hat on a peg near the door and stretched out on the narrow bench on his back, his legs bent and his boots plunked on the floor of the tack room. He laid his head on the blanket and gazed up at her green eyes.

"Is the day really goin' to come when it's this way every evenin'?"

"Soon." She nodded, brushing her fingers through his dark hair.

"I'd like to go to sleep and wake up on our wedding day. Wouldn't it be great if it were tomorrow?"

"No!" she protested. "I don't have your shirt finished."

"My what?"

"Shirt. Your shirt. Remember? I promised to make one for you."

"No ruffles!"

He blinked his eyes shut and lay motionless. His hands were folded across his stomach.

"Did I tell you the dress turned out terrific? Mrs. Franklin did a wonderful job! But you really need an extra-fancy shirt. I'm not sure why you don't like ruffles. They will make you look stunningly handsome."

One eye opened and seemed to glisten. "You go right ahead and talk, darlin'. . . . I'm just restin' my eyelids."

He scrunched his head back down into the blanket and closed his eye.

I've been talking, Mr. Tap Andrews, but I don't think you're hearing anything.

She rubbed the leathery wrinkles around his eyes. His muscles began to relax. Pepper continued to brush her hand across his face and hair.

Now is the time, Lord. I have to do it now!

"The Franklin baby is a little cutie, Tap. She's got a shock of dark hair just like her mother's. I wonder if our children will have blonde hair?"

She studied his face but didn't see any response.

"Look, Tap . . . there's something that's been eating at me for over a month. You know, I started to tell you on our way back from Denver . . . but it's just not easy to talk about. I don't want you to hate me, but I've got to talk about this before the wedding.

I promised the Lord I'd get this out while you still had a chance to change your mind."

She stared back at him and continued to rub her hand through his hair.

Are you going to sleep, Tap Andrews?

"Well, you'd better pay attention because I'm sure not going to get the nerve to talk about this again. I've been thinking about babies lately, I guess because of Rebecca Marie . . . that's the Franklin baby. Isn't that a nice name? We've never, ever talked about baby names, have we? Well, anyway, I suppose every woman thinks about babies when she's planning her wedding.

"I want you to know that I really do like children . . . and I'm scared to death to try to raise some myself. But I guess we'll learn together, won't we?"

Again she studied the peaceful face.

"Anyway, as I was sayin', I like children . . . but I once had a doctor tell me that it may be that I can't have any children. And it's only right that you should know that."

She pulled a handkerchief from her dress sleeve and dabbed at the corner of her eyes. Tap continued to lie motionless.

"Tap . . . I never, ever had anything so hard to say in my life. But . . . the reason I might not be able to have children is because I once had a miscarriage. I lost a baby once, Tap."

She stopped and took a deep breath.

"Now it was about four years ago . . . in Denver. That's why I didn't want to go back there. That's how I got involved with Dillard the first time. . . . No, he wasn't the father. I, eh . . . Tap, I don't . . . I don't know who the father was."

The tears streamed down her cheeks.

"Don't say anything until I finish." She put her fingers on his silent, motionless lips. "I told you there were some horrible things in my past that I was ashamed to mention. . . . Well, it doesn't get any worse than this. But I was sick . . . and I didn't take care of myself . . . and I was broke, and when I lost the baby, it was Dillard who paid the doctor's bills.

"Hardly a night goes by that I don't have nightmares about it, Tap. I'll live with those mistakes all my life. God's forgiven me, Tap—He really has. But I've got to live with the consequences of my past . . . and I guess you have to live with them, too—if you're willing, that is."

She was afraid to glance down at him.

"Look . . . just think about it. And we can talk later. Please don't leave me, Tap. Your coming into my life has been just about the only nice thing that's ever happened to me. There are a lot of women in this world, and lots and lots of them are surely more beautiful than me. Most of them are more virtuous than me, too. But there isn't a one of them that could love you more than I do."

She continued to brush his hair and stare at the stove. "Just you, honey—you're all I want in life. My Tap . . . and a peaceful house . . . with some—some laughing children. I don't want a big house on a hill or a place in Denver or Paris fashions. I just want the time and the place and the relationship to heal from the mistakes I've made with my life."

She took out the handkerchief again and blew her nose. Suddenly it felt oppressively hot in the room. Tap didn't move, but his face had a relaxed smile. She sat and stared at his chiseled features.

"What did you look like when you were a little boy? It's hard to imagine you as a boy. You were chasing around the streams of the goldfields of California while I was running down shady lanes of confederate Georgia. I wonder if we would have liked each other back then?"

She waited, but he didn't reply.

"Look, I'm changin' the subject—in case you hadn't noticed. Are you mad at me?"

Again silence.

"Tap, I think I just heard ten armed men ride up to the ranch. They're shootin' at the house!"

He didn't even twitch.

Lord, it's not my fault if he has hearing problems and fell asleep. I told him. I told him everything, just like I promised!

It was almost an hour later before she spoke again.

"Tap, the fire's going out. You want me to stick in some more wood?" She reached out and poked her finger straight down in the hardened muscles of his stomach. "Tap?"

Andrews reared up, then jumped to his feet, reaching for his revolver.

"What? Oh . . . Pepper . . . did I, eh, fall asleep? Am I glad to see you!" He wiped the cold sweat off his forehead and looked around. "I guess I was having a bad dream. Is it cold in here?"

"A little."

"Maybe I'll toss on a few more sticks."

"Certainly. Are you hearing better? I'm not yelling now."

"I think I can! It must have been that nap."

"What were you dreaming about?"

"I don't want to talk about it. It was . . . bad."

"Did you dream about me?"

"Yeah, but it wasn't . . . I mean, it was all my fault."

"What was?"

"The ruined wedding. We had to call off the wedding."

"Why?"

"I don't want to talk about it."

"That bad?" she asked.

"Yep. Sure makes a man feel good to wake up and know it never really happened."

"Did I, eh, say or do something?" she prodded.

"You sure did."

"Wh-what?"

"Oh, you dumped me because I forgot to come to the wedding."

"That was frightfully rude of me, wasn't it?"

"Oh, there's more."

"What?"

"I don't want to talk about it."

He stared at her green eyes for a moment and then broke into a smile. "Let's don't get so serious about a dream!"

Pepper took a deep breath and sighed. She stood up and walked over to him. Slipping her arms around his waist, she leaned her head on his chest. "I'm glad your hearing is better."

"Oh, there's still a little ringing in that ear, but I can hear you fine! I never want to go through that again. I kept on being afraid I would miss something important that someone was sayin'. Did I miss anything important?"

"Probably not." Pepper hugged him close.

"All right, despite the threat of being horsewhipped, I was sent out here to check on you two!" Stack's deep voice bellowed from the doorway.

"Hey, don't yell, partner. I can hear better," Tap announced.

"Just exactly what kind of treatment did the doctor give you?" Stack inquired.

"No, it wasn't—," she began to protest.

"Come on, you two. There's a little party, and it's getting kind of slow over there. Danni Mae and Wiley's been whisperin' in the corner, Rocky fell asleep in the rocking chair, and me and Paula and Selena's been playin' three-handed monte. If it gets much slower, we won't invite you two to come out to the ranch and see us again."

For the rest of the evening, Selena managed a running banter of jokes and innuendos, but she kept her distance from Tap as long as Pepper stayed at his side. The big card game at the table had Stack winning most of the pinto beans, and even Rocky seemed to be more agreeable by the end of the evening.

When Tap, Wiley, and Stack retired to the tack room in the barn, Pepper and Danni Mae decided to camp out by the fire in the front room. Paula and Selena headed to the bedroom, and Rocky climbed up the ladder to the attic.

Tap's ears crackled all night long. Several times he thought he heard something out in the barn. Each time he got up and wandered out into the dark stalls only to decide it was nothing and finally crawl back into his bedroll. By daylight he was cold, tired, and sore. But his right ear had drained some during the night, and he was able to hear much better.

While waiting for the women to stir around, Tap brought out Bob McCurley's horse and hitched it to the wagon. Then he drove the rig to the front of the house. Wiley fed the other horses and sauntered out to Tap, puffing steam from his mouth into the cloudy but frigid Colorado morning.

"You want me to ride along?"

"What for?"

"In case you run into that big-bore rifle again."

"I think he took a couple of pot shots and hightailed it to safety. I don't expect to see him until I get to the parlor at McCurleys'."

"I hope you're right . . . but you cain't trust anyone who throws lead from twelve hundred yards and never declares himself."

"Well, most times those types can't hit anything they're aiming at."

"Looks to me like he came close to you at the barn."

"Or it was just a coincidence I was standin' there. I'm not sure he could even see me from that distance."

"Hey, you two, good mornin'!"

Danni Mae stood at the doorway of the house. "You can't come in the house yet, but we do have some coffee ready." She held two tin cups in her hands. Her light brown hair was neatly tucked in combs, her lavender dress buttoned high on her neck, and she had an apron strapped around her waist.

Even Danni Mae looks like a ranch wife out here. Surprisin' how a change of scenery can make someone look so different.

Tap stepped over to retrieve a cup of coffee and left Danni Mae and Wiley visiting by the front door. He walked down the porch toward the east. Sipping the hot, slightly bitter coffee, he looked toward the barn and the dark sky that seemed to be hanging above it.

The tin cup was at his lips when he heard a report, and simultaneously a bullet ricocheted off the rock chimney about six feet from where he stood. Tap threw the cup to the ground and dove back on the porch.

A second shot roared in, crashing into the post holding up the porch roof. Tap drew his revolver and searched the trees behind the barn.

Wiley, also with gun drawn, scooted close to the windows and squatted down next to Tap. "Looks like he's back."

"But on a different side of the ranch. I've had all of this I want. I'm going to saddle up Brownie and go after him."

"What about Pepper?"

"You drive her back to McCurleys', Wiley. Tell her I'll be along later. No one is goin' to shoot at my ranch and just ride away."

8

Two more shots splintered the house. Then the gun in the woods fell silent. Using the barn for protection, Tap Andrews scurried to saddle Brownie while barking orders to the others.

"You reckon it was the same hombre?" Stack called. "He wouldn't need much of a gun to hit the house from those trees."

"It's not the same gun, but I don't figure two different men would fire random shots at the same ranch house, do you?"

"Don't ask me, partner." Stack held Brownie's reins as Tap finished cinching the saddle. "Gunmen seem to appear at your door like hobos at a widow's house."

Pepper scurried across the yard to the buggy.

"We're ready to roll," Wiley shouted from the yard.

Tap studied the trees behind the barn. Then he hurried over to where they were waiting. Wiley's horse was tied on behind the buggy.

Pepper reached down and put her hand on Tap's shoulder. "What are you goin' to do when you catch up with Little Bob?"

He squeezed her glove-covered hand. "If he shoots at me, I'll have to kill him, I expect."

"What if he doesn't?" Pepper asked. "What if he turns and runs?"

"Well . . . I, eh, I don't know. I'll think of somethin'. If we had a railroad around, I'd hogtie him and ship him home to Daddy. Anyway, I'll worry about that when the time comes."

The yellow-haired woman was covered with coat, cloak, and

hood. Still Tap couldn't miss the sweetness of her face or the concern in her eyes. "Pray about it, would you?"

"About what?" he asked.

"You know. What to do with Little Bob. You've got to do what's right in God's eyes, too."

"Well, you're really makin' it tough on me, girl. But you know it's not right to sit here and let him shoot up the ranch until someone gets hurt."

"I know. Be careful," she cautioned. "Tap, I expect I'll spend my life wonderin' if you'll make it back from somewhere. But I like that better than any alternative. When will you be coming by the hotel?"

"Tonight . . . tomorrow at the latest. In fact, I might beat you there. If this Little Bob character runs back to McCurleys', I might be waiting for you."

"That would be nice. Remember, you need to try on that shirt I'm sewing for you."

"You mean the ruffled one?" Wiley teased.

"How did you know that?" Tap demanded.

"Come on, Andrews. That's the only reason I'm stickin' around for the weddin'. Yes, sir, it's sure goin' to be some sight. Old Tap sportin' a bunch of ruffles. Say, you goin' to be packin' that Colt at the weddin'?"

"Yeah," Tap growled.

"No, he isn't!" Pepper scowled. "And the shirt will look quite comely. Mr. Wiley is obviously jealous."

"Well, partner," Wiley added, "I'll get her safe to McCurleys'. I'm going to hang around until tomorrow. If you don't come in by noon, I'll come out lookin' for ya."

"If Little Bob's back at the hotel, don't let him run off before I get there. And don't tell him I'm lookin' for him."

Wiley slapped the reins, and the drive horse trotted the buggy out of the yard.

Tap sauntered over to the front porch where Stack and Danni Mae were standing. "Is everything all set?"

"We'll take care of things here," Stack replied.

"Don't let the ladies wander around outside much until I take care of this bushwhacker. I don't want anyone to pick up a stray bullet."

Rocky stepped out to the porch. She was barefoot, and her uncombed hair hung straight down. Wearing only an oversized wool flannel man's shirt, buttoned crooked, she flung her arms around Tap's neck. "I don't like that Pepper woman! She's mean to me."

Tap peeled her arms from his neck and shoved her back inside. "Go get some clothes on, little sis." Then turning to Stack, he asked, "How much of that laudanum are you givin' her?"

"Just a sip in the evenin'."

"She's gettin' into something. Danni Mae, keep an eye on her. Maybe she has a stash up in the attic. And keep her away from me. I'm gettin' about as annoyed with her behavior as Pepper. I'd spank her, but I figure she doesn't need another man beatin' on her."

"You're right about that. April should never have taken her in. But what can you do with a girl like her? You can't kick her out in the cold."

"Maybe when you get to Laramie City, you'll find a place for her."

"Yeah," Danni Mae mused. "Maybe."

"I won't be home for a couple of days. Stack, don't go outside without packin' a carbine. If you ladies could, it would be grand to get the place cleaned up for the weddin'. We're expectin' about fifteen or twenty folks to come out—besides you all."

Danni Mae strolled with Tap out to Brownie.

"You might want to stay at the house," he cautioned.

"I need to talk to you. Tap, how well do you know Wiley?"

"As far as I can tell, he's a steady hand."

"How does he treat women?"

"Couldn't tell you that."

"I don't want to be with a man that treats women mean."

"You gettin' serious, Danni Mae?"

"Sort of . . . I mean . . . you and Pepper . . . and April's burnin' down. I want out, too, Tap. Wiley's sure talkin' sweet to me. He don't treat me like I'm workin' in a dance hall."

"You aren't, Danni Mae. You're just a ranch gal stayin' at a neighbor's house. You look good doin' this."

"Thanks. It feels good."

"By the way . . . Wiley thinks the sun rises and sets with you."

"You ain't kiddin' me?"

"Nope."

Her eyes began to mist. "This could be the best Christmas I ever had."

"It's a cinch it's goin' to be *my* best! See you in a couple days."

"Take care of yourself, cowboy. We're all countin' on you a lot more than you know."

He mounted the prancing horse, tipped his hat to Danni Mae, and spurred Brownie west.

This time Tap didn't skirt around the trail but rode straight at the trees where he figured the gunman had been hiding when he shot at the house.

There's no way Little Bob will hang around and face me down. I've seen his type. Fire a couple of shots and then run. That's his pattern. . . . I hope!

Tap's rifle lay across his lap, his coat pushed behind his holster. He tightened his gray, woven horsehair stampede string around his neck and pulled his bandanna over his nose and mouth to protect his face from the bitter cold.

Tap circled through the scattered piñon pines and scrub cedars that lapped across the clearing toward the barn until he found fresh tracks in the old snow.

"Brownie, those prints stand out like a shout in a cemetery. He was here, all right. A man could probably hit the house with a revolver from here, but I don't know if he was really tryin' to hit anyone in particular. He surely don't know a thing about hidin' his tracks."

The hoofprints led back into the trees and then swung southeast. Tap followed them keeping the gelding at a walk. One eye scanned the trees. His index finger wrapped around the cold steel of the cocked .44-40 trigger.

He patted the horse on the neck, then pushed his hat back, and scratched his head. "Brownie, this don't make sense. This pony's got smaller hooves and yet a longer stride than the one last night. Maybe Little Bob changed mounts. I just can't imagine why anyone would leave sign this easy to follow."

Tap assumed the tracks would swing back to the southwest and eventually toward McCurleys'. But he reined up when he hit the forest trail back to Pingree Hill.

He's goin' toward April's? There's no reason for anyone to head in that direction with the pass closed. Unless he didn't know the dance hall was burned down . . . or maybe he's lost.

Brownie hung his head low and trudged into the frigid wind as Tap spurred him up the forest trail. The tracks became harder to distinguish. Stack's wagon and several other hoofprints, including his own, still pocked the snow.

A small noon fire failed to warm him up. So Tap set his jaw tight to keep his teeth from rattling and pushed east on the trail.

He didn't turn off. That much I can tell . . . but I don't contemplate I'll be able to cipher his sign after we hit the main road. That's when I turn west and head for McCurleys'. As long as Brownie don't quit on me this time.

The trees thickened, and Tap spurred Brownie on up the hillside about twenty yards off the trail but parallel to it. The pace was slower, the snow deeper but less crusty, and Tap strained to detect any movement.

That trail down there would make an awful good place for an ambush. 'Course, I don't reckon Little Bob's got that figured out yet. But there's a few pieces of this puzzle that just don't fit.

He found he could now hear Brownie's hoofbeats, but with the increased hearing came incessant itching. He constantly rubbed his right ear and face. The daylight dimmed, they plodded even more slowly, and Tap grew colder.

Lord, a man could freeze to death bein' this cautious.

He finally spurred Brownie to the top of a ridge that overlooked what was left of April's dance hall. Leaving Brownie in the trees, he scooted across an outcropping of snow-covered rocks and surveyed the scene.

The road looks dead. No horses in the corral. Could be one in the barn. The road out to McCurleys' is empty. The south road is clear. I guess I could have stayed on the forest road.

A slight movement to the right caught his eye. He pulled the bandanna down to his neck and strained to see through the evening shadows.

There's a horse down there at the head of the forest trail. Someone's waitin' for me after all! You're a more patient man than I gave you credit for, Little Bob.

By staying on the ridge back in the trees, Tap avoided revealing his position to the road through Pingree Hill. But such caution prevented him from seeing who waited for him.

His fingers frozen, Tap pulled off his spurs and shoved them into his saddlebags. Then he left Brownie eating the bark off an aspen tree and hiked to the point of the bluff. From that position, behind the cover of a juniper tree not more than eight feet tall, he spotted a man, carbine in hand, slouched behind the last rocky outcrop before the descent into Pingree Hill, poised to shoot down the forest trail.

The only way to keep out of sight is to go down that grade of rocks and boulders. It's kind of hard to keep your rifle aimed when your boots are slippin' on ice.

The trip down the grade was tedious. Tap stopped at each step to make sure the man hadn't spotted him. By the time he made it to the bottom of the rocks, sweat rolled down his forehead and froze in the wrinkles around his eyes.

One shot in the back would drop him, but that's not exactly what I promised Pepper.

Tap lifted his Colt with his right hand; his left still carried the Winchester. He inched his way closer. He could see that the man sported a worn black canvas coat and black beaver felt hat. Then the man, using his carbine as a crutch, struggled to his tethered horse, dragging his right leg.

He's hurt pretty bad, and I haven't even fired a shot! Looks like he's fixin' to leave. Brownie's too far away to try to chase him.

Tap slipped his revolver back into the holster and slapped the '73 to his shoulder.

Keep your head down, old horse . . .

The metal sights were only two inches above the horse's ears when he squeezed the trigger. As he expected, the blast sent the horse galloping down the incline toward the barn at Pingree Hill. But what Tap didn't expect was that the man was able to retrieve his carbine and fire two quick shots at Tap as he dove into the rocks for cover.

That's not Little Bob! That looks like . . .

The second shot sprayed granite slivers into the right side of Tap's face, and the pain racked his ear.

Jimmy Ray? What in the world are you doin' out here?

Two more quick shots from the carbine kept Tap pinned down. As soon as there was a pause, Tap rolled to the right and came up on his knees. With bullets flying to the left of him, he leveled the rifle as Jimmy Ray staggered straight at him still firing wildly.

Nobody's crazy enough to run straight into a rifle!

Jimmy Ray plowed ahead. The bullet from Tap's .44-40 caught him in the right side of the chest. The shot lifted him off the ground and slammed him into the rocks near the head of the trail. He tried to rise to his good leg, then fell facedown into the snow.

Tap approached the gunman with caution, keeping his rifle cocked and pointed. Jimmy Ray struggled to raise his head. Kneeling by his side, Tap rolled him over on his back and propped his head on a rock.

"Jimmy Ray, you didn't give me much of a choice."

Spitting blood, he cursed Andrews. "You killed me last week, you . . ."

Tap noticed the bandaged leg. "You let it turn to gangrene? I told you to tourniquet it, keep it cold, and see a doc. What did your friends do, desert you in a hot cabin?"

"They never came back. Did you kill them, too?"

"I left 'em in Rico Springs—pretty much alive."

"Don't leave me out here in the snow. I hate the cold. Take me down to the barn. You owe me!"

"I owe you?"

"You chased off our cows, shot me down straight away, and

then stole our poke. You owe me! Don't leave me up here for the wolves. Bury me down there at Pingree Hill."

"Can't promise you anythin', Jimmy Ray. The ground won't thaw for three months."

"The barn . . . bury me in the barn. You know it ain't frozen."

"I don't plan on . . ."

Tap stopped talking as Jimmy Ray was overcome with coughing. Then, with a deep guttural growl, he collapsed into silence. Tap didn't bother checking his pulse. He hiked back up the bluff and retrieved Brownie. Returning to the dead outlaw, he dismounted and lashed Jimmy Ray across Brownie's rump. He could see Jimmy Ray's horse waiting near the barn as he rode slowly down the grade toward the dance hall ruins.

Lord, I didn't want to shoot Jimmy Ray—and I surely don't want to try to bury him. Maybe the ground under the dance hall will be soft enough to dig. I don't have to go down very far. It'll be dark in an hour. I'll need to hit the trail . . . or maybe stay in the barn.

He stopped by the burned-out dance hall and stared through the evening shadows at the rubble.

Maybe there's a piece of a shovel left in this mess.

He turned Brownie toward the barn.

I don't understand why he didn't take care of that wound. I don't understand why I get drawn into these things. I don't understand who shot at the barn last night. Jimmy Ray didn't have the range with that carbine. Took his cows? They were Rafter R beef. Shot him point blank? He was tryin' to kill me! Stole his poke? His poke? He wasn't even at Rico Springs with the others. How did he know what happened? He must have talked to them. . . . That means Karl and the others are here!

Tap dove into the charred wreckage of April's dance hall just as bullets flew at him from the barn. Brownie bolted up the road, Jimmy Ray's body bouncing behind the saddle.

Not finding much cover, Tap dragged himself through the soot of the kitchen. Bullets whizzed overhead with gun smoke encasing the road between him and the barn. Suddenly his right leg broke through the charred remains. Tap's foot dangled into what was left of a root cellar. He jerked his leg free and dove behind one of the three rock chimneys that stood as proud memorials in the rubble. Bullets ricocheted off the rocks as he tried to determine the direction of each of the shots.

Jimmy Ray, I'll have to hand it to you. Most men get real honest when they're dyin', and you lied to the end. Makin' a suicide run at me and then askin' to be buried in the barn. That would have been real nice—me hefting Jimmy Ray's body and the boys shootin' holes in me.

His eyes surveyed the ruins, looking for a way back up Pingree Hill. He jammed his hat on a rock that had tumbled off the fireplace and ran his fingers through his dark brown hair. After a heavy barrage of gunfire, Tap fired off several wild shots at the barn and dove back out into the middle of what was left of the kitchen floor. The gun smoke provided enough cover to slip down into the root cellar.

Tap figured that the burst of bullets from the barn were cover for someone to break out to the north and circle around the dance hall ruins. Two other guns fired an occasional bullet, but it was obvious they were just waiting.

Scrunched down in the ruins of the root cellar, Tap stared up at the darkening gray sky that flickered through the broken, burned timbers overhead. He pumped his Colt with six cartridges from his bullet belt and tried to wipe the black smudges from his face.

I've got to narrow the odds. If I can bring down one of 'em and keep the others back for half an hour, it'll be dark enough . . . maybe.

It was several minutes later that he finally heard a man shout from behind the privies. "He's gone! He ain't there, Karl! He ain't in the dance hall."

"He's got to be," Karl shouted.

The voice sounded like it was coming closer. "Well, he ain't!"

"Maybe he's dead. Is he lyin' there dead?"

"Nope. There ain't no one here, I tell you. . . . Come see for yourself!"

"You check it out."

The man cautiously approached. Tap crouched down lower.

Come on . . . come over here . . .

Two quick shots rang out, and Tap raised his revolver and pointed it toward what he could see of the sky through the timbers.

"Did you get him?" someone in the barn yelled.

"Nah. It's just his hat. He must be laying dead in these timbers, but I can't see him. Come on out, boys, and give me a hand finding him."

The barn door squeaked open, and boot heels stomped toward the dance hall.

Not yet. I don't need all three of you yet.

Suddenly Bufe's tattered black hat came into view. Then he stared down into the charred timbers and spotted Tap. He raised his gun, but the blast from Tap's .44 Colt sounded quickly, and Bufe tumbled into the blackened ruins.

"He shot Bufe!" someone shouted.

"Where is he? I don't see him!"

"Gun smoke's over there in the corner."

"I don't see anyone."

"He cain't jist disappear!"

Three more shots were fired in Tap's direction as he hunkered down and waited for the others to come closer.

"You get him?" It sounded like Karl's booming voice.

"Just his hat. I can't see him. . . . Where is he? He must be over there."

"Ain't nothin' over here but ashes and charred wood."

"Maybe he's back at them outhouses. He could be using that rifle."

"If he were back there, we'd be dead by now! He's in here. We seen the gun smoke."

Tap heard some shuffling of position and muffled conversation.

"You go up to the privies, Hank. I'll stay here, and we'll wait him out."

Karl, if you think I believe that!

The acid smell of charred timbers all around him forced Tap to keep rubbing his mustache and nose to keep from sneezing. It seemed as if half the kitchen had collapsed into the root cellar. He eased around behind a burned beam and leaned against a dug-out dirt shelf lined with glass jars of moldy fruit. From this spot he could barely see the top of the barn across the road.

"Are you all set?" Karl hollered.

Hank's not at the privies, but I don't know where he is. . . . Come on, boys, make a move.

The snap of a charred timber caused Tap to look up in the shadows to the right.

"Hey! Here he is!" Hank shouted. His first shot down through the ruins broke a jar of fruit by Tap's left shoulder. Tap's bullet caught Hank in the neck. Hank's second shot fired wildly toward the barn, but he was dead when he dropped to the ashes.

A barrage of bullets ripped down into the six-foot-by-eight-foot root cellar. Tap tried to crawl behind more timbers and turned around with his back against the dirt floor. Glass jars shattered everywhere. Beams shifted and started to collapse from the weight of Hank's body.

I've got to get out of here! I'll be buried alive! Lord, I hope Karl's still on the fireplace side of the building.

Shoving a timber aside, Tap pulled himself to the end of the cellar to stairs carved into the dirt. He pushed himself straight up out of the ashes and fired two quick shots toward the kitchen fireplace. There was so much gun smoke he couldn't tell where the surviving gunman was. He dove out of the ruins into the snow-packed yard. Two bullets struck the ground behind him. In one motion he rolled to his knees and fired at Karl. The gunman held a revolver in each hand but peered back into the smoke.

The bullet hit Karl in the center of the chest below the rib cage. He staggered back but managed to fire two shots at Tap. The first ripped through the left shoulder of Tap's coat, slicing deep into the muscle like a branding iron. The second hit the dirt in front of him. Karl slumped to his knees.

Tap's final shot slammed into the gunman just above his right eye. The big man flew backwards, collapsing motionless in the ruins.

Andrews stood to his feet and gasped for breath. He pulled off his rolled burgundy bandanna and stuck it under his coat to stop the bleeding. It was almost dark, but he could see that his coat and trousers were covered with soot and ashes, except for a splattering of rotten peaches—and a red streak of blood oozing from his shoulder.

I've got to get Brownie!
I've got to get cleaned up.
I've got to get to McCurleys'!

Weak and weary, Tap staggered up the road east where the gelding waited, Jimmy Ray still strapped to his back.

After six steps, Tap crumpled to one knee. He forced himself back on his feet and took a few more steps. He heard the creak of a wagon and a shout from the south. Tap spun and tried to raise his Colt.

"I don't know what's goin' on here, mister, but don't raise the pistol. I've got some buckshot in this scattergun that will split you in two!" a voice shouted.

The wagon rolled closer as Tap caught his breath. A woman drove it. A man with a shotgun sat beside her. Tap tried to wipe the soot and sweat from his eyes. He gawked at the two in the wagon.

"Rena? Wade?"

"I should have known!" the woman's voice roared. "Underneath that filth is Mr. Tap Andrews, I suppose."

"Am I glad to see you two!" Tap replied. He took one more step toward the wagon . . . and fell on his face.

Everything was a bit blurry and disorienting for a while. Tap knew that Wade Eagleman helped him to the barn where he lay back in the hay and caught his breath. Rena poured some burning liquid on his shoulder wound and then bound his shoulder with a sack and the bandanna. Without any water, she gave up trying to clean him.

Tap was sitting up, trying to gingerly put his coat on when Wade came back into the barn.

"Well, Andrews, I'm glad it's gettin' dark. I won't have to look at you. Come on, we're drivin' through the night to reach

McCurleys'. The way it's threatenin' to snow, we need to keep movin'."

"What about all this?"

Wade shoved his wide-brimmed black hat down tight and tugged on some leather gloves. "You mean the bodies you left lyin' around?"

"Eh . . . yeah."

"You know a man named Kasdorf?" Wade asked.

"He's got a farm and a whole passel of daughters south of here."

"That's the one."

"I don't really know them, but Pepper does."

"Well, Kasdorf rode up to see what all the shootin' was about. He offered to come up tomorrow and see that they get buried. Meanwhile, he's takin' their horses to his place to wait for someone to claim them. So come on. I've got Brownie tied behind the wagon, and Rena has plenty of blankets. Let's go deliver you to that blonde beauty of yours."

Wrapped in a green quilt, Tap crawled up next to Rena. Wade drove the rig west. The outline of the road could barely be spotted in the snow-reflected darkness. Tap pulled the blanket clear over his hat in the back to keep the frigid breeze off his neck.

Rena spread a big buffalo robe over their legs. They rattled alongside the mountains of northern Colorado for an hour without talking much.

"I still don't know what you two are doin' out here," Tap finally commented.

"Rena didn't tell you?"

Her raven hair tucked in a fur hood, Rena wore her wool blanket like a veil around her face. "No, I didn't tell him anything. The way he was mumblin', I figured he'd forget everything and just ask us later. Andrews, you're a walkin' disaster. Did anyone ever tell you that you seem to attract trouble?"

"Yeah. There's this yellow-haired lady out on the North Platte that keeps remindin' me of it. Not to mention a banker's wife down in Globe City, Arizona. Anyway what's a half-breed lawyer and the queen of Denver doin' out here?"

Wade's deep voice boomed above the creak and rattle of the wagon. "I got your telegram."

"And what's Rena doin' here? I thought you went back east."

"I changed my mind."

"Why?"

"With Victor dead, I had nothin' to run from. Besides, I took a fancy to the barrister."

"You and Wade? You've got to be kiddin'!"

"What's that supposed to mean, paleface?" Eagleman jibed.

"I mean . . . I just didn't . . . you know. It's just that you're, eh—"

"Come on, Andrews." She poked his ribs with her elbow. "Get yourself out of this one."

"I, eh, think you'll make a perfect couple. Why, you two might even want to think about getting married some day!" Tap blurted out.

"Too late for that," Rena replied. "Do you see this?"

"What?"

"My ring."

"I can't even see your hand."

"If you could see it, you would see a very nice wedding ring."

"Wedding ring?" Tap choked. "You two got married? When?"

"Three days ago."

"Well, I'll be. . . . I can't believe this. I mean . . . this is great . . . I think."

"We needed to settle some matters, so we took the south pass and swung around here hoping to make your wedding on our way to Arizona."

"Oh . . . yeah . . . our weddin'! Oh, man, I've got to get to McCurleys'. I've still got a few days 'til the wedding, right?"

"What are you talkin' about, Andrews?"

"I've been dreamin' about bein' late for the weddin', and sometimes you and Rena were the ones who made me late. This is like it's prophetic. I've got to get to McCurleys' tonight."

"Relax, Tapadera. Just a little nervous before the big day, are you?"

"Did you say you're goin' to Arizona?"

"Wade's goin' to take me down to Globe City and let me tell the judge my side of the story. He thinks he can get it cleared up."

Tap poked his head completely out from under the blanket. "You mean, get that sentence of mine dropped?"

"At least the murder charge. I'm not sure how they'll handle the escape from A.T.P.," Wade replied.

"There's another reason we came." Rena paused. "I just had to see if that blonde wildcat could really sink her claws into you. I do hope I'm invited."

"Of course you're invited. Pepper will be pleased. Pleased that you're married!"

Only the dim reflection off the snow from a very dark night gave hint of where the road was, but the wagon rolled along quickly on the frozen road. Its rattles and creaks were the only sound for miles.

"Do you know of a cabin between here and McCurleys' in case this storm hits?" Wade asked.

"Nope." Tap pulled back the blanket from his neck. It stuck to the dried blood and peach preserves splattered on his jacket. "The quicker I get cleaned up, the better."

It got too cold to talk. All three seemed content to hunker down and brace themselves against the weather. Tap drifted in and out of sleep, thankful that the wind was blowing at their back.

Lord, if I had my life to live over, I'd just be a lawman. At least I'd get some pay for the gunfights and ambushes. I'm sure not doin' a very good job at running away from trouble.

Suddenly Tap sat up and poked Eagleman, who was dozing off with Rena's head on his shoulder.

"Wade, what about that bank note on the ranch? What can I do about that?"

Eagleman transferred the reins from his left to his right hand and brushed his long black hair off his turned-up coat collar. "If you can find a way to satisfy that bank note, well, that means they're admitting your ownership is legitimate. 'Course, they can just call in the note and repossess the ranch at any time if you don't pay. About the best I could do was come up with a debt repayment plan for you—how you'd pay this note off at a higher rate of interest over a three-year period."

"You think they'll go for that?"

"I don't think banks want to own property out in the wilderness. They'll make a good return on their investment, but they have to wait a little longer than usual."

"Can you go tell the bankers that?" Tap asked.

"Not me. I'm on my way to Arizona, remember? But I did draw up some papers for you. I suggest you and Pepper take a honeymoon trip and stop by that bank in Ft. Collins."

"Thanks, Wade."

"I didn't say it would work. I just said it was worth tryin'."

"How much farther to McCurleys'?" Rena asked in a quiet, sleepy voice.

"Two long hours at a minimum," Tap projected.

It was closer to three hours, almost daylight, when the wagon containing three frost-covered, teeth-chattering passengers finally rolled to a grating, rattling stop in the yard of McCurley Hotel.

9

After sleeping on the floor at the ranch house, Pepper savored the big feather tick in her room at McCurleys'. Little Bob Gundersen was at the hotel, so she expected that Tap would be along quickly. She was disappointed that he had not arrived yet, and she had gazed out her window at the cloudy, cold sky to the north most of the afternoon. She day-dreamed about a quiet ranch house with no one around for miles except her and Tap. After the sun set, she decided that he must surely be waiting until morning.

It was still dark outside when she awoke, but she lay in bed on her back with the flannel sheets tucked snugly around her neck.

I figured on moving all my things out to the ranch on Thursday . . . then come back to the hotel. But with a house full of people, there's no reason I couldn't spend those few days at the ranch. Mr. and Mrs. McCurley will bring the reverend on Friday.

Maybe Tap went back to the ranch last night. Did I tell Danni Mae to keep Selena away from him? Two more days, Mr. Tap Andrews. Surely you can wait two more days!

A sharp rap at the door startled her. She sat straight up, then pulled a flannel sheet up around her shoulders.

"Yes?"

"I need to talk to you about Tap." It was a soft, feminine voice, yet it belonged to a woman who expected others to obey her commands. Pepper couldn't place it, but something gnawed at her stomach.

"Just a minute. I'll get my robe. . . . Who are you?"

The voice now boomed with the authority of a dance-hall madam. "What difference does it make who I am or, for that matter, what you're wearing or not wearing? You want to know about Tap, don't you?"

Oh, no. Not her!

Pepper rushed to the door, dragging her robe in her left hand across the cold, polished wooden floor. She slung open the door and stared at the brown, catlike eyes of a tall, slim, raven-haired woman, still dressed in cloak, hat, and gloves.

"Rena!"

"How charming you remember me."

"What are you doing here?"

"You do want to know what your Tapadera went off and did, don't you?"

"Is he all right?"

"Oh, you know Tap. You could run a train over him, and he'd say he's all right. Most of the bullet holes seem to be in his hat. Spending time with that handsome, brown-eyed man is never boring, dear. Is it?"

Pepper tried to straighten her hair with her fingers but still felt tacky as she stood at the doorway barefoot in her flannel gown. "Don't 'dear' me! What are you doing with Tap? You don't have any business with him!"

Rena tugged off her left glove and stuck the hand in front of Pepper. "Do you see this ring?"

"So what?"

"Well, honey, I'm happy to announce that I just got married!"

"You're what?" Pepper gasped. "You—you . . . Tap . . . I . . . it can't . . ."

"Tap?" Rena laughed. "That would be like marrying a hurricane, and you know it. I married Wade Eagleman."

"You did? When?"

"Last week."

The knot in her stomach unraveled.

The pain in her chest melted.

The tenseness in her neck relaxed.

"Tap's out in the barn. He wants you to bring some bandage cloths, towels, and hot water."

"Is he shot? Where did you find him?"

"Wade and I are going to get some breakfast from Mrs. McCurley. Tap can explain everything. And listen, Pepper, I figure there are only a half-dozen really good men in the whole West. I got one of the good ones, and you got another. That leaves all the other women to wrangle over the few left. I presume our fighting days are over. What do you say?" She reached out her bare hand to Pepper.

"You're really married to Wade?"

"I really am."

Rena's hand felt cold, strong, and rather bony as Pepper shook it. "Tell Tap I'll be right out! I've got to get dressed."

She pulled on a deep blue dress and quickly laced her high-top black shoes. Then she stopped at the dresser mirror and stared at her hair.

Yellow hair. Everyone envies yellow hair. I envy the woman whose hair is always orderly . . . like Rena's.

She brushed her hair back but decided against setting it in combs. Then she rushed to the hotel barn carrying towels over her shoulder and a bucket of steaming water that she had hastily retrieved from the kitchen.

Tap teetered back by the far wall dressed in oversized duckings. His suspenders hung at his waist. He was bare-chested and bent over, trying to push a comb through his matted brown hair. A bloody, raw wound gaped on his shoulder. His face and hands were covered with black soot.

"Tap! What happened?" She hurried to his side.

"It ain't much, really. I came out mighty lucky."

"But how? Little Bob's here at the hotel."

"Yeah . . . well . . . I ran into that other bunch."

"What bunch? What are you doing?"

"Trying to comb the glass out of my hair."

"Glass?"

"Yeah. From the jars of peach preserves."

"Preserves?"

"I was in the root cellar at April's."

"I thought it burned down."

"That's why I'm covered with ashes and soot."

"What about your shoulder? Did you get shot?"

"Only cut a little furrow. Didn't bury any bullets, if that's what you mean."

"Who did this?"

"That bunch that burned down April's. They shot at the house, suckered me down the trail, and tried to ambush me at Pingree Hill."

"What happened to them?"

"I shot 'em."

"All four of them?"

"Yep."

"Dead?"

"Yep."

Pepper leaned her head over and took a deep breath. She felt dizzy and faint.

Tap stood up and grabbed her shoulders. She raised her eyes to his.

"I'm going to be a young widow. It's okay. Me and the Lord have already discussed it . . . and I consider any time He lets me have with you is better than none at all."

"Well, don't bury me yet, darlin'. I aim to live a long and happy life with lots of children."

But I told you it might be I can't . . . Lord, I just can't tell him again!

She stepped back and looked him over. "Whose trousers are those?"

"Bob McCurley's. Mrs. Mac insisted on takin' my gear and washin' it out. But she forgot to bring a spare shirt. Maybe you could get me one."

"After I get you cleaned up. Sit still. I'm not even sure you really are Tap Andrews."

"You know some other guy who comes in lookin' like this?"

Through all the grime and blood she saw Tap's incredible smile and the flash of his eyes that she knew had stopped the hearts of hundreds of dance-hall girls throughout the West.

"Not really." She took the rags and washed the dried blood off his shoulder and back. Almost an hour later she poured the last of the water over his freshly washed hair.

"Now if you promise not to freeze to death, I'll run get you a shirt. Dry your hair with these towels."

"I won't freeze, but I figure I'll probably fall asleep right after I grab some breakfast."

"You can sleep in my room. I'll go down to the kitchen and help—"

"For two more days I'll sleep in the barn. After that . . ." He gazed at her dancing eyes. "We're really goin' to do it, Miss Pepper."

"Which? Really going to wait or really going to get married?"

"Both."

"Yeah. It feels good to do it right, doesn't it?" she added.

"Yep. Now . . . how about grabbin' me that shirt?"

"Be right back!" Pepper sprinted out of the barn and returned within minutes.

"Mrs. Mac said I should apply this ointment to your wound and then wrap it with these cotton rags."

"What is that stuff?"

"Something she bought from Red Shirt."

"Who?"

"Some Ute down near Durango. Folks around there say it cures everything from lumbago to bee stings and bullet wounds."

"It don't smell too pretty."

"If you're worried about smelling pretty, you can use some of my perfume." She stuck her ear up by his face. "Do you like it?"

"Get behind me, temptation!"

"Control yourself, cowboy." She rubbed the ointment into the wound.

"Ahhh! Good grief, that stuff stings!"

She twisted his ear. "Sit still!"

"Are you twitchin' me like a horse?"

"It worked, didn't it?" She grinned. She wrapped strips of white cotton cloth on his shoulder. "Now try on your new shirt."

"Not the ruffled one! Listen, I don't have to try it on until the weddin'."

"It's the only shirt around here that has sleeves long enough for your arms. Now go on. Try it on. I figure if you wear it around today, you'll get used to it."

"I am not wearin' that shirt!"

"You promised."

"I said I might consider it on our weddin' day, but we ain't gettin' married today. So go fetch me another shirt."

"I'm doing nothing of the kind. You are going to wear this shirt, Mr. Andrews. I worked hard to make this for you."

"I'd rather wear this blanket than that shirt."

"Well, that blanket will look right nice in the hotel dining room!" She stormed out the barn door and stomped across the yard to the hotel.

Tap was sound asleep on the hay when Wiley kicked his bedroll. "You fixin' on hidin' under them covers all day?"

"My clothes dry yet?"

"Nope, but they're hangin' by the woodstove in the kitchen." Wiley handed him a tin plate and cup. "Here. I brought you some coffee, eggs, and biscuits."

Tap eased to his feet and took the dishes. Slumping on the end of a bench, he stuffed a buttered biscuit into his mouth.

"You goin' back to the ranch?" Wiley asked.

"After I get my clothes and a nap," Tap mumbled.

"You don't intend on leavin' that yellow-haired girl mad at you, do you?"

"She wanted me to wear that ruffled shirt right into McCurleys'."

"Seems to me some gals is worth it, Tap. That one you got jist might be one of 'em."

"She knew I wouldn't wear it. I don't know why she tried that stunt on me."

"Well, I'll tell you what," Wiley continued. "I'm goin' on out to the ranch. There's a brown-haired beauty that I'm a missin'. Now if you want to leave Pepper in there with that little weasel Bob Gundersen tryin' to gum up the works, well, then you're about as gal-dumb as you are gun-smart."

"He's doin' what?"

"Makin' himself a pest, as far as I can tell." Wiley guided his horse out of the stall and began to saddle it.

Tap paced the floor of the barn and twice started for the hotel wearing a wool blanket over his otherwise bare shoulders. "Before you mount up, Wiley, how about fetchin' my clothes for me. I don't really care if they're dry or not."

"You'll get rheumatism wearin' wet clothes."

"Well, I'm not waitin' any longer."

"I'll be back." Wiley smiled and walked his horse over to the hotel.

Tap dug through his gear, pulling out his holster. He checked the chambers of the Colt.

"You call for your laundry?" He spun around to see Pepper standing at the door. "It's still wet, you know."

"Listen, Pepper, I'm sorry I carried on about the shirt. I've been thinkin'. I'll wear it at the weddin'. I promise. But not today."

"Well, I had a little talk with a married lady, and she told me not to push you so hard."

"You talked to Mrs. Mac?"

"No. To Mrs. Eagleman."

"Rena? You and Rena are on speakin' terms?"

"Actually we have a lot in common."

"Sure. You're both good-lookin', sweet-voiced, and pig-headed."

"Oh, I bet you say that to all the girls! Here. You can wear these wet clothes if you want to. But please don't die of pneumonia until after the wedding."

"Where's my jacket?"

"It's still wet. Come on over to the parlor. You can stand by the fire."

"Where's Little Bob?"

"In the parlor."

"Is he pesterin' you?"

"Depends."

"Depends on what?"

"On what you call pestering."

"What did he do?"

"He asked me to go hunting so he could show me his new rifle, and he wanted to give me a present—a gold hat pin."

"What did you tell him?"

"No."

"No to which? The ride? Or the hat pin?"

"Both, of course."

"I think it's time I had a serious talk with Little Bob."

"I think it's time you got dressed." She handed him the garments and retreated to the hotel.

The long johns were dry, but the shoulder looked permanently bloodstained. The pullover gray flannel shirt, though tattered, was dry and clean. The ducking trousers felt heavy and damp.

Tap, hands and face already cold, hurried to the hotel. The heavy, dark clouds hadn't dropped any new snow. At each step there was a crunch of snow and a jingle of his spurs. Reaching the front door, he pushed his hat to the back of his head, resat his Colt in the holster, and then swung the door open.

A blast of heat rolled across the room from the roaring fire in the fireplace. A woman touched his arm.

"Pepper, where is . . ." He glanced at the heavy-lipsticked smile. "Rena?"

"Pepper's in the kitchen, Tap. She told me to send you that way. I think she's trying to avoid Little Bob."

"Where is he?"

"Oh, he's right over . . ." Rena searched the room with her eyes. "I guess he's gone to the kitchen, too."

"I'll take care of that!"

"Be careful, Tap. You shoot down a character like that, and Daddy will have old Allan Pinkerton and his sons on your trail for the next thirty years."

"I don't plan on shootin' him. Just figured I'd run him off."

"He won't chase," Rena cautioned.

"You think he's that brave?"

"No. I think he's that dumb. Believe me, I've seen the type. And so has Pepper."

"You two are a lot alike."

"She mentioned you said that." Rena smiled. "I presume you meant we are both demure, witty, and sophisticated."

"Eh, something like that. Now I think I'll go put this Romeo in his place."

Tap wished he hadn't strapped on his spurs as he jingled toward the swinging doors of the hotel kitchen. Slipping the door partially open, he saw Pepper at the chopping block and Little Bob, with his back toward Tap, waving a butcher knife at her.

Moving quickly across the gray-painted floor, Tap drew his revolver. With one movement he grabbed Little Bob's shoulder-length blond hair and jerked his head back, shoving the .44's barrel under the man's chin.

"Drop the knife, Little Bob!"

Tap heard the utensil clunk to the floor. "Wait . . . I was just . . ."

"Actually, Tap, Little Bob was . . . ," Pepper began.

"Little Bob," Tap shouted, "do you know what would happen if I pulled this trigger right now?"

"Tap!" Pepper cautioned.

"Do you know?" Tap demanded.

"Eh, I guess . . . you'd . . . kill me," Little Bob stammered.

"Actually, the bullet would enter your neck with a little hole about the size of your little finger and then—"

Pepper tugged at his arm. "Tap!"

"Then it would exit right out the top of your head about the size of a grapefruit. And what little brains you have would be splattered up there on the ceiling. Now I'm goin' to do you the biggest favor of your life. Rather than force Miss Pepper to look at your empty skull, I'm turnin' you loose. I suggest you ride out of here within thirty minutes. If you don't—we'll have to ship you home to Mama in a pine box!"

Tap shoved Little Bob toward the swinging doors. Gundersen stumbled into the parlor and then scurried up the stairs.

Pepper looked at Tap with disgust. "Well, Mr. Andrews, Little Bob has been an extreme pest, but it so happened that he was helping me slice potatoes. That's why he had the butcher knife. Do you plan on takin' his place?"

"He was what? But I thought you said—"

"Oh, he's a jerk. I'm glad you scared him off, I guess. But he wasn't trying to hurt me."

Tap looked down at the revolver. "Well, he got the point anyway."

"You weren't going to shoot him, were you?"

"Not with an uncocked pistol still sittin' on an empty chamber. I just wanted to encourage him some to leave."

"He won't go, you know. He's too spoiled to run off."

"Spoiled."

"You know—a rich kid who's always gotten everything he wanted. He's too blind to run."

"That's just what Rena said."

"She's a smart lady. Pretty, too. And has good taste in men."

"What is this with you and Rena? Last time you were together, you wanted to claw out each other's eyes."

"Look, Rena and me both figure we'll be young widows someday, and we'll need a good friend."

"But she just drove in this mornin'. How could you possibly decide all of that in just—"

"Mr. Andrews, what you don't know about women is appalling!"

Tap began to laugh. "Darlin', you keep right on surprisin' me. I like that. There's nothin' routine about Miss Pepper Paige."

"And don't you forget it, cowboy. Now what are you planning on doing when Little Bob doesn't ride off?"

Tap sidled up to the cookstove to dry his canvas trousers. "I'll ride out to the ranch and forget him, but that leaves you here."

He slipped his arms around her waist. "How about you just comin' to the ranch and spendin' the final days waitin' out there? Wade and Rena have a wagon. You can ride out with them."

"In case you forgot, you have a houseful already."

"That's the point. A few more cain't hurt. We'll just make pallets for everyone."

She wrapped her arms around his neck. "Actually, I was thinking the same thing. I can't get everything ready to move out until tomorrow, but if we're both at the ranch, nothing can go wrong before the wedding, can it?"

They stared at each other. Pepper grimaced.

Wade Eagleman, black hair flowing down the back of his leather coat, banged his way into the kitchen.

"Come on, you two," he chided. "Tap's got work to do."

"What kind of work?" Pepper asked, releasing Tap and stepping back.

"Little Bob is calling Tap out."

"Oh, you've got to be joshin' me!" Tap moaned.

"I told you he wouldn't leave."

With Pepper holding his arm, Tap walked out to the parlor.

"Well, where is he?"

"Out on the porch." Bob McCurley pointed. "I wish that stage route was open. I'd just coldcock him and send him to Santa Fe."

"Has he got a gun?"

"I don't know what he has." McCurley shrugged.

Tap and Pepper strolled out to the porch. Little Bob Gundersen stomped straight up to Tap, holding a pair of tan leather gloves in his right hand. He raised the gloves and swung them at Tap's face.

Andrews caught Little Bob's right wrist with his own left hand, then swung a right cross that caught Gundersen in the chin with a loud crack that caused his head to jerk straight back.

Little Bob would have fallen to the porch had it not been for Tap's strong grip on his wrist. When Tap finally released him, Gundersen staggered back against the porch rail.

"You didn't do it right!" he cried.

"Well, I sure wasn't goin' to stand around while somebody slapped me."

"That's not the way it's done!"

"What's done?"

"A duel. I challenge you to a duel!" Gundersen cried out.

"A duel? Have you been readin' those dime novels?"

"I challenge you to a duel for the hand of Miss Pepper Paige!" Gundersen called out.

"Little Bob," Pepper threatened, "this has gone far enough! If you shoot Tap, I'll kill you myself."

"You see, son, it ain't worth your while!"

"Don't 'son' me! What's it going to be—dueling pistols or swords?" Gundersen wiped his bleeding mouth on the back of his trembling hand.

Tap glanced at Pepper and shook his head. "Darlin', you see what you've gotten me into?"

"Me?"

"If you'd shot him two weeks ago, I wouldn't have to do it today."

"So it's dueling pistols?" Little Bob's voice quivered.

"I didn't say that. We will duel—with rifles at six hundred yards."

"What?"

"You can hit something besides the broad side of a barn with that Winchester '76, can't you?"

"I don't have a '76. It's a Sharps 'Creedmoor.'"

"But it's a .45 caliber, right?"

"It's a .44-90 . . . but I haven't shot it much."

Someone used a '76 to shoot the barn! If it wasn't Little Bob or the Pingree Hill boys, then who?

"Well, whatever. Get her loaded up," Tap demanded.

"But you can't . . . I can't . . ."

"If you want to back out, Little Bob, just grab your saddle and ride. This duel wasn't my idea."

"I'm not backing out. Gundersens don't back away from anything."

"Then they must all be dead."

Pepper pulled at Tap's shirt sleeve. "You aren't really going to do this, are you?"

"Get your fancy rifle, boy. Let's get this over."

Within minutes the hotel guests had bundled up and emptied out of their rooms to stand in the frigid, cloudy Colorado morning to watch. Wiley and Eagleman stepped off the six hundred yards along the river.

"Here's what we'll do," Tap instructed Little Bob. "I'll hike down there to the south, and you go north. Wiley, you go with him to make sure he's on your mark. Wade will see that I'm on mine. When I get all set down there, I'll take off my hat and wave it back and forth above my head. After you see that, you wave your hat to signal you're ready. Then Bob McCurley will fire his gun into the air, and the duel begins."

"But . . . it's too far. Neither of us will hit anything from there," Little Bob protested.

"You've got twice the powder I have. You just need a little more confidence, son."

"Tap, this is crazy!" McCurley complained.

He marched up to the hotel owner, looked him straight in the eye, and winked. "If this man wants a duel, he'll get a duel!"

It took several moments for both men to get into position. Tap could see Pepper and Rena standing arm in arm on the porch of the hotel.

"Look at the two of them, Wade. You'd think they were long-lost sisters!"

"Well," Eagleman responded, "neither of them have anyone much in this country but you and me. I don't suppose that's all that reassurin'. What have you got planned?"

"I'll show you."

Tap flipped up the sights of the upper tang long-range sights and adjusted the vertical screw, then the windage bar. He cocked the rifle and took off his bullet-riddled gray hat, waving it back and forth above his head. Holding his rifle to his shoulder, he waited several moments.

Finally he saw Little Bob Gundersen take off his hat and start to wave it high. As he did, Tap squeezed off a round. The smoke drifted forward, partially blocking the view.

"You shot him before the signal?" Wade choked.

"Nope. I shot the hat."

"But he dropped. I saw him go down."

"Maybe a heart attack . . . but I didn't hit him."

"How do you know?"

"I wasn't aimin' at him."

Tap moseyed toward the crowd that now circled Little Bob, who lay unconscious in the snow. Bob McCurley and Wiley were laughing as the others stared in shock.

"No . . . he's all right, folks," McCurley reassured them. "He just fainted. When Tap put a bullet clean through the center of his hat, he must have got real nervous and just passed out. Get me them smellin' salts, Mama. I'll bring him around."

Pepper and Rena joined Tap and Wade.

"Well, thanks for not killing him." Pepper nodded. "I've definitely decided to ride out with Rena and Wade. They offered to bring me and my belongings out in the morning. You think there's room for all of us at the ranch?"

"We'll go out and make room. Wiley, you ready?"

"Saddled and waitin'. Ain't you goin' to tarry until that boy comes around?"

"Nope. He's liable to try somethin' even dumber. It's what I get for wantin' to marry such a handsome woman. You goin' to be all right 'til tomorrow?" he asked Pepper.

"Little Bob won't come within six hundred yards of me." She smiled.

The wind whipped their faces, and neither Tap nor Wiley said much all the way back to the ranch. As they crossed the frozen river, a few flakes of snow drifted down. By the time they reached the barn, the snow blew hard sideways, reducing their vision and cutting flesh.

Stack Lowery met them at the barn. "What happened to you?"

"You should see the others."

"Dead?"

"Yep."

"You bring this storm in with you?"

"I guess. . . . Hope Pepper will make it out in the morning. She's decided to stay here until the weddin'. You'll never guess who's comin' with her."

"The governor?"

"Wade Eagleman and Rena. He and Rena got married!"

"Well, I'll be hanged. It's like an epidemic."

"What?"

"This marriage thing. I surely hope it's not contagious. Right, Wiley?"

Wiley led his horse to an empty stall. "How are the ladies?"

"You mean Danni Mae? She's fine. Rena and Wade—ain't that somethin'? It's almost providential."

"What's providential?"

"Havin' a lawyer drivin' to the ranch."

Tap walked over to Stack. "What are you hintin' at? What's goin' on?"

"We had a visitor while you were gone."

"Who?"

"Said his name was Blackstone."

"From the Rafter R?" Wiley asked.

"That's the one."

"What did he want?"

"To give you this."

"What is it?"

"A Notice to Vacate."

"What do you mean?"

"As far as Danni Mae and me can cipher, the bank that owned the mortgage on your ranch sold the note to Ed Casey. And Casey wants to take possession in ten days."

"Over my dead body!"

"That don't seem to concern him much. Maybe Wade can give you some advice. There's one other thing you ought to know," Stack informed him.

"Rocky's run out of laudanum?"

"Besides that."

"What else?"

"Blackstone's packin' a big, new '76 Winchester in his scabbard."

Tap stared off toward the north as Stack handed him the papers.

"Welcome home, partner."

10

Tap Andrews read the NOTICE TO VACATE ten times. Every time it came out the same. Fighting Ed Casey had purchased Hatcher's loan note from the Fort Collins bank. According to the papers, Casey had paid off the loan and taken legal possession of the Triple Creek Ranch. There was no provision for Tap to raise the money, and the NOTICE TO VACATE would be enforced on January 1 by duly appointed agents of the Larimer County Sheriff's office.

Selena brought coffee as Tap, Wiley, and Stack huddled at the big dining table in the front room. Her long, black hair glistened from a recent washing. Her eyes sparkled. "Maybe you shouldn't be in such a hurry to get married, *mi caballero* . . . I mean, if you're going to lose this ranch and all," she purred, fluttering her eyelashes. She stopped behind Tap and began to massage the back of his neck. "You need to relax more!"

Danni Mae's brown curls bounced on her shoulder as she whisked through the room. She grabbed Selena by the sleeve of her purple velvet dance-hall dress and tugged her across the room.

"Hey, what are you doing?"

"Come on, Selena, we've got to clean up this place including the attic."

"Why?"

"You heard Tap. Mr. and Mrs. Eagleman are coming out with Pepper in the mornin'. We might have to sleep more people than

Rocky up in the attic. Besides, we have to have the whole place weddin'-clean. That's almost as much work as funeral-clean!"

"I don't do domestic cleaning!" Selena pouted.

"You do now!" Paula chimed in. "We're guests here. It's Pepper's house. I mean, it will be Pepper's house."

Tap watched the women scurry around for a few moments.

Stack Lowery rolled up the sleeves of his plaid flannel shirt. "Sometimes it starts feelin' like the dance hall on a quiet Sunday afternoon."

"Wiley, I've got to go up and talk to Fightin' Ed. How do you think I can do that without him tryin' to take a potshot at me?" Tap reached inside his shirt and rubbed the scarred furrow of the bullet wound on his shoulder that now ached and itched at the same time.

"Sneak up and hogtie him, I suppose. He's a mighty determined man once he makes up his mind. I surely don't figure he'll want to talk to you much."

"Will he be at the headquarters?"

"This close to Christmas he might be in Cheyenne already. He has a big house there, you know."

Tap leaned back in the wood-slat chair and threw up his hands. "This whole thing is gettin' to be a mess."

"Maybe Eagleman can go up there with you and straighten it out. I hear he's a mighty good lawyer."

"No, he's got to go to Arizona. He's goin' to try to settle that matter in Globe City for me."

Stack locked his big fingers and stretched his hands behind his head. "You know, Andrews, if you wouldn't get yourself into these fixes, you wouldn't be in such sorry shape."

"I always surmised I'd have to live with the consequences of my actions. I just hoped they wouldn't all come due on the same day."

Wiley swished his coffee dregs around in his cup and then gulped them down. "Tap, what I can't figure is that if Fightin' Ed has the ranch already, why did Drew take potshots at the place? I mean, if it was Drew. I reckon even Fightin' Ed can wait a few days to have you run off legal-like."

"Maybe I'll ride up to the border tomorrow and deliberate the matter with Drew myself."

Wiley glanced at Stack, then back at Tap. He shook his head. "You and Drew sittin' down and discussin' somethin' civil? That will be the day. Stack, did you ever meet a man who riles up hombres into a fightin' mood quicker than Tap Andrews?"

The big man with the square-jawed face grinned from ear to ear. "Nope. But then I never hung around John Wesley Hardin, Stuart Brannon, or any of them."

With chatter and giggles from the women at the other end of the room and in the attic, Tap strolled to the front door.

"Looks like I need a new hat." He poked his fingers through several bullet holes in his old gray beaver felt.

"You going for a ride north?" Wiley asked.

"Thought I might ride out and look around."

"You won't get far in this storm."

"With more company coming in the mornin', I need to make sure all the bushwhackers have cleared out."

"I'll ride with you," Wiley offered.

"No need for that."

Wiley rose from the table and meandered toward the door. Although several inches shorter than Tap, he was just as broad-shouldered. "Look, Andrews . . . old Stack here, he's used to livin' in a house full of women. But it kind of gets on my nerves. So I think I'll ride along and make sure you don't get lost before the weddin'."

"Well, come on, Wiley. We might as well ride out there and freeze. I don't reckon I've been warm since Yuma."

Within fifteen minutes they were plowing into the blowing snow. Peering over his bandanna, which was wrapped around his face and ears, Tap squinted into the storm. Wiley followed slightly behind and to the right of Tap and Brownie. They rode straight north with the storm at their right side.

"What are we lookin' for?" Wiley shouted.

"Some ambusher's tracks, I guess."

"You ain't gettin' nervous about the weddin', are you?"

"What's the weddin' got to do with this?"

"Nothin'. That's my point. You jist cain't sit still for ten minutes, can ya? We're out here freezing our tails lookin' for tracks that's been covered up by snow. It's like lookin' for a whisper in a tornado."

"You can turn back anytime," Tap hollered.

"That ain't the burr. What I'm hintin' at is, you and me both know we ain't goin' to find anything in a storm like this. So why are we really doin' this?"

Tap looked over at Wiley, who was trying to hunker down into his coat. He didn't say anything but kept riding.

That's a good question. It's just . . . It can't be . . . I can't lose this ranch. Me and Pepper have all our dreams tied to this place. I want it bad, Lord. I know I don't deserve it, but the truth is, You've been givin' me better than I deserve for quite a while now. I don't figure I'd need much else for a long time. This place would keep me out of Your hair. I'll work hard for it, Lord. You know I will.

When Tap's eyes caught a mound in the snow ahead of them, he pulled the rifle from his scabbard and stepped out of the saddle all in one motion. Brownie stood motionless, slumped into the storm, the reins dropped to the ground, the tapaderas plastered white with snow.

"What is it?" Wiley shouted.

Tap brushed the snow off the brown and white mottled hide. "One of my heifers . . . shot through the neck with a big-bore rifle!"

"How long ago?"

"Can't tell . . . frozen stiff . . . about an inch or two of snow. So my guess is that it was Drew Blackstone on his way north after servin' those papers."

"You figure he shot others?"

"I reckon, but most of 'em hang out down closer to the barn."

"That one will still butcher."

Tap nodded his head. "Yeah, but not 'til we thaw it out."

"What do you figure on doin'?"

"You uncoil that *reata* and throw a loop on her. She'll drag on top of the snow all the way to the ranch. Hang it in the barn, and we'll chop her up for the weddin'."

"You headin' north?"

"Yep."

"You need any help? Blackstone don't exactly play by the rules."

"There ain't no rules when someone starts shootin' cattle. They're tryin' to take the whole ranch, but the bovines belong to me. No one rides in here lead-droppin' cows."

"You can't find him now. It's gettin' dark. Let's go warm up. We'll check it out tomorrow."

Tap stared straight at Wiley's brown eyes. "I let you stay at my house and eat my food, and now I have to listen to your naggin'?"

"You know I'm right."

"Look, I'm just ridin' up here a few more miles, and then I'll turn back. If I'm not back by dark, it'll only be a little later."

Wiley slipped from his saddle and tied a double half-hitch around the dead cow's hind legs. "Well . . . go on. I don't reckon you ever listened to anyone in your life. I didn't figure you'd start now." Wiley remounted, dallied the *reata* to the saddle horn, and started back to the ranch.

Tap watched Wiley slide the heifer southward. Then he turned Brownie into the wind and snow and spurred him northeast. A half hour later he found a cow and yearling shot and covered with snow. After that he couldn't find any cows, downed or alive, nor did he spot any trail. Everything was covered with fresh snow, and it was miserably cold.

Just before dark Brownie quit.

No matter that Tap spurred him, the gelding refused to ride into the storm any longer.

"Brownie, you can't quit now!" he hollered. "Yee-ahh! Git up! Git goin'! Come on, boy!"

The horse didn't budge.

First Wiley, now Brownie. You're gangin' up on me, Lord.

"I ain't through with you, Blackstone! Don't you ever think you pulled one on me!"

Tap swung Brownie's rear to the storm. The gelding trotted south.

Oh, sure, any old nag can turn tail and run for the barn.

That evening most of the house guests crowded around the fireplace or the piano. Tap sat in the rocking chair and kept the fire stoked. He thought about the NOTICE TO VACATE, dead cows . . . and Pepper.

Mostly, he thought about Pepper.

"You ain't singin' much, cowboy." Selena leaned close to his ear as she wrapped her arm across the back of the chair.

"I'm not much of a singer."

The dark-eyed Selena lifted his hand. "You want to dance?"

"I don't dance much either."

"I know you don't drink. So what in the world do you do?"

"Yeah. What do you do?" a soft voice echoed.

Both Tap and Selena turned to see Rocky scoot up next to them. Her long, straight brown hair was tangled. Her eyes were red and raw.

"If you're lonely, I can make you feel better," she offered.

"Little sis, you shouldn't be talkin' like that!" Tap scolded.

"Don't call me 'little sis.' I ain't little. I can do anything Selena can do. And some of it, I do better!"

Tap reached over and took Rocky's thin white hand and pulled her in front of him.

"I call you 'little sis' as a compliment. You're a pretty girl. If I had a little sister, I'd treat her just like I'm treatin' you."

"I don't want to be your little sister," she pouted.

"I know it. And I'm tellin' you right now, that's the best I have to offer you. Pepper's my girl, and even Princess Selena knows she doesn't have a chance. That's why she teases me so. Right, Selena?"

"He's right, Rocky. And remember, I told you there's a whole lot of cuter men than him up in Laramie City."

"Well . . . why don't we go to Laramie City now?"

"We'll be there in a few days. This is a good time to rest up. By next week we'll be having parties every night," Selena promised.

"Do they have drugstores in Laramie City that sell laudanum?" Rocky asked.

"On every corner."

"I don't feel so good."

Tap noticed dark circles under her eyes. "You need to eat something, little sis." Tap released her hands. "I haven't seen you eat a thing all day."

"I've been sick. I ain't hungry."

"You go over there and try to eat something," he insisted.

"Will you dance with me if I eat something?"

"Eh, yeah . . . sure. If you promise not to laugh at me."

Rocky scurried across the room.

"How about me, Mr. Gunfighter?" Selena ran the fingers of her right hand up Tap's arm and across his chest. "Will you dance with me if I go eat something?"

"If I dance with you, Pepper will kill us both, and you know it!" He glanced back at Rocky. "She doesn't have much to look forward to in this life, does she?"

"She's what we call a *mariposa*," Selena whispered.

"A butterfly?"

"Yes. She is beautiful but frail. Life span is short."

Sometime around nine o'clock, Tap waltzed around the room with a smiling Rocky. Then he, Stack, and Wiley headed for the barn.

Tap slept fitfully, dreaming of being late for the wedding. He chased cattle rustlers through deep snow.

And butterflies.

He woke up tired and cold.

After breakfast he, Wiley, and Stack gathered on the front porch. Small flakes of snow drifted down lightly.

"I'm goin' out and push my cows down toward the barn before any more get shot."

"I'm goin' with you," Wiley offered. "You ought to be here when Pepper rolls in."

"No need for two to freeze. It won't take me and Brownie more than an hour."

"And then a few hours ridin' north to see who shot those cows of yours. And then chase the bushwhacker clear to the Wyomin' line. And a visit to Laramie City or Cheyenne! Right, Stack?"

"It's been known to happen."

"All right, all right. You can come along and baby-sit! Stack, tell Pepper we're tendin' cattle and hope to be back before noon. Shoot, we'll probably be home before they get here."

"You want me to feed the horses?"

"I'd appreciate it. If we get more company, I'll have to build a bigger barn."

"How about a dance hall and hotel?" Stack teased.

"Not me! I aim to have a peaceful and quiet place here."

Within two and a half hours Tap and Wiley had circled behind most of the longhorns. Wiley drove three cows out of a stand of leafless aspens and joined Tap with the herd.

"You got enough feed in that meadow for them to winter out?"

"That's what I aim to find out. Longhorns will paw through the snow better than those whitefaces."

"Ain't that the truth! Do they count out right?"

"I'm missing a couple still. Maybe they'll get lonesome and wander in."

"They could be shot."

"Yeah. I'm tryin' not to think about that."

Wiley pointed to a rider galloping through the snow from the south. "Is that old Stack ridin' up to help us?"

"That house full of women must have chased him out."

"He's ridin' pretty fast. Maybe something happened to Pepper!" Tap spurred Brownie toward the oncoming horse.

"Tap, we got trouble!" Stack shouted. "Rocky's gone." He had the collar of his fleece coat turned up and his tan felt hat pulled down and fastened by the stampede string.

"What do you mean, gone? I thought she was sound asleep in the attic when we left this mornin'."

"That's what we calculated. But when Danni Mae finally went up there, she and all her blankets were gone. You and Wiley don't have that blaze-faced horse of yours, do you?"

"Onespot? He's in the corral with the others . . . isn't he?"

"Nope. I think she took him."

"You find tracks?"

"Pretty much snow-covered."

"You think she headed out during the night?"

"Could be."

"But I was awake most of the night!"

Stack pushed back his hat and wiped his forehead. "The snow makes a quiet cover."

"She could freeze to death."

Wiley rode up to the others. "What's the problem?"

"Rocky ran off in the night. Go ahead and run those longhorns back to the meadow north of the ranch house. Then stick around and tell Pepper what's going on when she comes in. Stack and me will go out and try to cut Rocky's trail."

Tap spurred Brownie to a trot and headed southeast toward the Medicine Bow Mountains. Straight east of the barn they found tracks.

"You reckon those are Onespot's tracks?"

"Yeah . . . that's a good guess. But she's been out here a long time. It wasn't snowin' all that hard last night, and yet those tracks have almost disappeared.

They followed the old tracks in the almost two-foot-deep snow. Brownie plowed through the drifts with his long, high stride as Tap tried to trace the indentations. The snowflakes turned wetter and increased in size. Visibility dimmed to twenty or thirty feet.

"It's warming up enough to really dump some snow," Stack hollered.

Tap pulled his bandanna down away from his mouth.

"Where would she go, Stack?"

"I know she don't have any kin. April tried to send her home, but there wasn't any. There's no tellin' where she's headed. To a drugstore to get more laudanum, I reckon."

"What town?"

"Well, the only one we've mentioned is Laramie City."

"You figure she'll head north?"

"If she knew which way was north."

"I'm losin' these tracks. . . . There's no way of followin' her now."

"Maybe we ought to branch out and cover more ground."

"Yeah. You ride right up the draw, and I'll take the tree line. I'll see you at the cedars."

"Where?"

"Follow the edge of the chaparral north for a few more miles, and you'll find a day camp in a cedar grove. I'll swing through the trees and meet you there. If we haven't found her by then, we'll have to turn back . . . and leave her in the Lord's hands."

"If she made it that far north, she might be in Wyomin' by now."

"I hope she found someplace warm. I'm about numb."

The snow continued to pile up, and Tap lost all sign of hoof-prints. He followed what he knew was the high trail to the Wyoming border, hoping Onespot remembered the way and carried Rocky to that point.

On the ridge overlooking the cedar grove, Tap saw nothing but falling snow. Even the evergreen trees looked indistinct on the white horizon.

He was within thirty feet of the tightly clumped scrub cedars when he saw the outline of a horse tied to a tree.

Onespot! She's here! Rocky made it to the cedars!

Tap slid off his saddle into the knee-deep snow and plowed toward the trees.

"Rocky! It's me—Tap. Rocky?"

A snow-dusted mound back under the cedars caught his eye.

No . . . no! She's too young. She's . . .

Tap shuffled through the snow. He brushed the snow off, then gently folded back the wool blanket.

Rocky lay curled up in a fetal position. Her eyes were closed. She looked asleep. She was already frozen stiff.

Tears traced his face and froze before he bothered wiping them off. He looked her over and found no bullet wounds. In fact, he found no marks on her. She was clothed in her oversized dance-hall dress and hooded cloak and wrapped in two blankets.

He plopped down in the snow and laid her blanket-covered head in his lap, patting it tenderly. "Little Sis, you didn't get many breaks in this life."

Lord, she didn't need to run away. Maybe . . . maybe if I hadn't pushed her away every time . . . maybe if I would have said nice things . . . Lord, I don't know why this had to happen! She didn't even live long enough to get a fair shake.

"You in there? Tap!" a voice knifed through the storm.

"Stack?"

"Yeah."

"Come on in!"

"I saw Onepenny. Did you find her?"

"Yep."

"She dead?"

"Yep."

Stack stepped off his horse and shuffled through the snow toward Andrews. "Was she shot?"

"No . . . she just . . . got cold and went to sleep. You know how it goes. Did you hear some shootin'?"

"Nope. But you've got a cow dead back in the draw. Shot this mornin'."

"Big bore?"

"Yeah."

"Then Blackstone's out here!"

"I reckon." Stack pulled back the blanket and looked at the girl. "Rocky, darlin', if you'd only stayed at the house. I promised to take care of you!" Stack let the blanket back down and turned away from Tap. "I'll take her back with me. Are you goin' after Blackstone?"

"Seein' Rocky like that . . . I just don't have the heart for it." Tap sighed. "He'll be in Wyomin' before I could catch him. I reckon I'll ride back with you and see that Little Sister gets buried proper."

"I'd appreciate it, Tap. She surely took a likin' to you. It's a shame, ain't it? She should be laughin' and gigglin' and goin' to school and church socials and all that. There ain't nothin' good about this. Maybe I should never have brought that laudanum back to her."

"She would have run off sooner. She had to make her own choices . . . I guess."

They mounted up and rode south with the blanket-wrapped Rocky cradled in Stack's strong arms.

There wasn't much enthusiasm at the ranch when the men
returned. Even the arrival of Pepper, Wade, and Rena was a muted
reunion. Pepper and Tap had a few minutes of privacy to discuss
the details of the wedding day. Not long after supper, the men
headed for the barn, and everyone went to bed.

No one got much sleep.

On Wednesday the men dug in the frozen ground until noon.
They buried Rocky beneath the cedars behind the barn. Bundled
up and blanket-covered, they all gathered around the grave.

Danni Mae sang.

Stack eulogized.

Paula read some Bible verses.

Tap prayed.

Everyone cried.

The men rode out in the afternoon and brought back plenty of
pine and cedar boughs for the girls to beautify the house for the
wedding. While the women whirled around the room decorating,
the men took to the tack room early after supper.

"Wade, in all reality what can I do about Fightin' Ed?"

"Shoot him."

"What?"

"If you killed him and got away with it, chances are no one else
would pursue the matter. Now I didn't say that it was legal, moral,
or biblical . . . but it would work."

"Well, how about a suggestion that is legal, moral, and
biblical?"

"The only thing you can do is go to him, tell him you want to
keep the ranch, offer him a schedule for repayment of the loan . . .
and then see what he says."

"What if he refuses?"

"There's absolutely nothing you can legally do. He's legally got
a right to buy a note that is past due and take possession. Even if
you were Hatcher, you'd lose the place."

"So you're sayin' that it all depends on Fightin' Ed's good
nature?"

"Yep."

"You ain't got one chance in hades," Wiley asserted.

"Do you think I should look for a lawyer in Cheyenne?" Tap asked.

"A lawyer won't be able to do a thing. If I thought it would make a difference, I'd go there with you myself," Wade replied. "I reckon I can do you more good in Arizona. Frankly, the only thing that will save your ranch is a divine miracle."

"That's better than no chance at all! It would break my heart to lose this place. But it was Hatcher's hard work that provided it, not mine. Guess I'll have to wait for that miracle."

The floor was hard.

The room cold.

The night long.

Tap thought daylight would never come.

But it did.

And so did breakfast . . . chores . . . more conversations with Pepper . . . and at about 11:30 A.M. the double report of a rifle fired far up to the north.

Everyone was in the house when Tap heard the muffled explosion roll down to the ranch. He immediately saddled Brownie and rode up the draw. Within an hour he was at the northern edge of his herd of longhorns. One cow was dead, another wounded and struggling. Tap put her down with his Colt. Then he circled north into the trees and finally cut a fresh trail heading straight for the Wyoming border.

So you're goin' home for Christmas, Blackstone? Not if I catch up!

The clouds began to dump their load. The snow fell with big, wet flakes the size of four-bit pieces. Within half an hour Tap was soaked to the bone. Within an hour, there was no sign of the trail north at all.

Tap refused to think about quitting the pursuit. He pushed, kicked, spurred, and threatened Brownie through the storm hour after hour until he reached what he thought was the pass that led into Wyoming.

I don't know if he's ahead of me . . . or behind me.

"Well, I guess it's time to go home, Brownie. If we don't head back now, we'll end up like Little Sister."

The blizzard erased all sense of the time of day. Tap stopped on the way back to build a warming fire and give Brownie a break. He huddled over the smoldering sticks for a long time, but the whistling wind and the wet snow combined to make a miserable fire.

"You might as well give it up, gunslinger!" the voice behind him shouted.

Tap didn't bother turning around but stayed crouched over the fire.

How in the world did I let him slip up on me?

"Yeah, Blackstone, it ain't much of a fire."

"I wasn't talkin' about the fire. I was talkin' about the ranch. There ain't no way you're goin' to keep it."

"You sure aren't the one who's goin' to take it away from me. I thought you had shot your quota of longhorns and went runnin' back to Wyomin'. I didn't reckon you'd face me. 'Course, you aren't exactly facin' me now."

"You can turn around. I ain't afraid."

Tap slowly turned and stared through the snow at Drew Blackstone's cocked .45. He was about fifteen feet behind Tap. In the edge of his vision, Tap could see a waiting horse.

"It was nice of you savin' me another trip down to the ranch. I do believe Fightin' Ed just might give me a bonus for shootin' you."

"Fightin' Ed sent you to kill me?"

"Nah. He thinks the sheriff will have to evict you. But I figure if I get the job done ahead of time, I jist might make foreman of this Colorado operation."

"So you keep coming down and taking potshots at my barn and my cows?"

"Your barn, your house, your cows, and you, Andrews. What a shame if one of those big bullets just happened to plug you. I figured you'd come out after me days ago. In fact, I'd all but given up doin' anythin' more than pop cows. But now you walked right into my sights. It's sort of like an early Christmas present."

"You think you're good enough to kill me with one shot?"

"I guess we'll find out. You aiming to pull leather?"

"Have I got any other choice?"

"Not that I can think of."

A clump of heavy, wet snow slid off a tree limb high above Drew Blackstone and plopped into the snow behind him. The gunman jerked his head slightly. Tap pulled his Colt and fired all in one motion.

Blackstone's gun went off at the exact same time. But his bullet sailed to the right.

Tap's didn't.

The impact of the lead caused Blackstone to stagger back and fire again, but by this time Tap had dived into the snow behind a cedar tree. From behind the trunk he cautiously glanced across the little clearing. He couldn't see Blackstone.

Did I drop him? Maybe he's layin' dead in the snow.

Tap waited behind the trunk as the snow continued to fall. Finally, he peered around the tree. A bullet crashed above his head and sent him diving back into the snow. As he came up, ready to fire, he heard the whinny of a horse and the creak of saddle leather.

He's tryin' to ride out of here!

Tap ran to Brownie and swung up into the saddle just as Blackstone disappeared into the snowstorm about thirty yards ahead. He spurred Brownie to follow but reined up after only two steps.

It's just vengeance, isn't it, Lord? I already chased him off my ranch, but it's not even mine anymore. I'm just mad. Mad at losin' the place. Mad at Fightin' Ed for not leavin' me alone. Mad at Blackstone for his arrogance. Mad at that bunch for burnin' down the dance hall. Mad at Little Bob for badgerin' Pepper. Mad at myself because Rocky died, and I couldn't do a thing about it.

A man can't live on anger alone, Lord. It's a lousy life. I won't do it anymore! You take care of this, Lord. Blackstone. Casey. The ranch. All of it. There are just some things I've got to learn to let You handle.

This is one of 'em.

I've got more important matters.

His thoughts turned to Pepper and the wedding.

I'm not goin' to mess it up for her now.

The snow continued to pile up, and the frigid wind blasted his back as he rode through the darkening storm back down the slope of Medicine Bow Mountains. He pulled his hat low and slumped his shoulders, trying not to block any more of the storm than necessary. His eyes were almost squinted shut. His left eyelashes froze together, and he didn't bother opening them up. He couldn't keep his teeth from chattering.

This is stupid, Lord.
Really stupid.
What am I doin' out here on a day like this?
Cowboy pride.
It's a deadly disease.

He knew he was losing direction and could only trust Brownie's instinct. They groped for hours to find the ranch house. He began to be afraid they had ridden past it in the storm.

Finally, in the blinding snow he thought he saw movement in the trees. Pulling his Winchester, Tap dove off the saddle into the snow and rolled to his knees. With the '73 cocked and pointed at a rider who suddenly appeared, he was startled to hear a voice holler from the right.

"Tap, if you don't put that gun down, we're liable just to ride back to the ranch and leave you out here laying in the snow!"

11

"Wade?"

"Yeah, me and Stack and Wiley were sent out here by the women to make sure you didn't try to sneak out of gettin' married! Where have you been?"

"I was chasin' a cow-killer!"

"Stack, I believe he's so nervous he's delirious," Wade teased as the three snow-covered men rode closer.

"I reckon you're right about that," Stack's voice boomed. "Kind of like a kid the first time they set foot in a dance hall, if you know what I mean."

"All right, all right!" Tap stood to his feet and brushed the snow off his chaps. "You had your fun. You're all lucky I didn't pull the trigger."

"Andrews, in all your life, did you ever pull the trigger blind—without knowin' your target?" Wade pressed.

"Eh . . . no. But this could have been the first time."

"Are you goin' to mount up and come home to that yellow-haired girl, or do we have to rope you and drag you in like that dead heifer?" Wiley chided. "You been actin' mighty peculiar."

"Peculiar? I just tracked Blackstone to the state line."

"You shoot him?"

"I think I winged him . . . but he rode off."

"And you let him go?"

"I just didn't want to . . . press it any further," Tap stammered.

"That's what I mean. Tap Andrews lettin' a bushwhacker ride

out alive. He's not in his right mind, boys. Coil your *reata,* Wiley. Let's hogtie him before he makes a—"

"I'm mountin'! I'm mountin'! It's too hangin' miserable to argue with you three."

"You can say that again," Wiley roared. "There's five of the purdiest women in the state of Colorado back in that warm house. Why in the world are we sittin' around out here in this blizzard?"

Wiley led the way home. Wade trailed behind. They made sure Tap rode in the middle with Stack alongside. The trip back to the ranch went quickly, broken up with jokes and jibes mostly at Tap's expense.

When they reached the barn, they stalled the horses. Tap went into the tack room and lit a fire in the woodstove. He stood there alone for several minutes trying to dry out.

"You boys want to come warm up before supper!" he hollered.

There was no answer.

Stepping to the barn door, he shouted, "Hey, I've got a fire blazin' in here!"

Did they all go to the house already?

"Stack? Wiley? Wade? You up in the loft?"

He ambled to the middle of the barn and stared around at the flickering shadows. Someone tackled him from behind. Both men crashed to the dirt floor of the barn. Tap reached for his holster, but the .44 was gone. Kicking wildly with his boots, he caught the man in the shins, but it didn't budge the big man off his back.

"Hogtie him, boys!"

"Stack? What are you doin'?"

Wade Eagleman stepped out of the shadows and tied Tap's bandanna over his mouth as Wiley tied his feet.

"Wha-at doya . . . ," Tap tried to mumble.

They bound his hands and feet.

"Hiss is eel unny. Cut me oose!" he hollered.

"The old boy seems to have a speech impediment," Wade chided. "Well, I guess he's ready for delivery. I'll open the door if you two want to heft up the merchandise."

Stack and Wiley grabbed the lashed Tap Andrews and carried

him out of the barn and across the yard. Tap entered the house on their shoulders.

"You know there's nothin' more attractive than a man roped and tied!" Danni Mae teased.

Paula studied him. "Well, they ain't much for dancin', but you always know where to find 'em!"

"They hardly take up any room. Why you can just pile two or three of 'em over in the corner," Rena laughed.

"Well," Selena said giggling, "the next time I'm in Denver, I'm goin' to buy a couple for myself."

"Miss Pepper, here he is. Where do you want him?"

"Well, boys, the wedding isn't until tomorrow, so just toss him over by the fire someplace. I'll take care of him later. I'm a little busy right now tryin' to get supper ready for this whole crew."

"Eery unny! Un-ie ee!"

"Did you know that he mumbles like that?" Wiley remarked as they plopped Tap down by the fire. "You might want to trade him in on one that talks right."

"I'm sure I can straighten out his speech problems," Pepper asserted.

"Ey!" Tap tried to holler.

"Stack, it's kind of noisy in here. How about you playing the piano? I think a little party music might be appropriate."

"Old it!" Tap insisted.

"Paula, could you set the table for nine?"

Selena waltzed over to where Tap was bound. "Is she just going to throw him away? Why, if nobody wants him, I'll take him. Stack, would you help me toss him in the bedroom?"

"You touch him, and you'll be sleepin' in the snow tonight. Do you hear me, Selena?" Pepper shouted across the room. Then she turned to the men at the door. "All right, Wiley, cut him loose— if he promises not to leave the yard until after the wedding!"

Selena winked at Tap. "What a shame, *mi vaquero*."

Tap stood up rubbing his wrists. "You boys are really funny," he pouted. "You dang near cut off my circulation."

"What a crybaby," Pepper teased. Her bright green dress made her blonde hair look like pure gold. "You would have done the exact same thing to them if they were the ones getting married tomorrow."

Tap stared at her for a minute. He looked around the room. Everyone waited for his reaction. Suddenly a wide grin swept across his face, and he began to laugh. "Yeah, but it's a lot more fun when it happens to someone else!" He glanced at Stack. "Well, don't just sit there, Mr. Lowery. Play something on the piano for us!"

Tap walked over and gave Pepper a long hug. "Looks like you captured me."

"It was only partly a joke. I don't want either of us leavin' the yard until after the wedding."

"Well, sure . . . I just . . . you know, need to ride out and check the cows in the mornin', but that's not goin' very far. You wouldn't have any objection to—"

"Not a chance," she insisted. "You're not leavin' the yard until you say the vows, and that's final!"

"We'll talk about it later," he muttered looking around at the others in the room staring at them.

"Do you honestly think I'll change my mind?"

"Eh . . . no, I don't reckon so."

"You're absolutely right, Mr. Andrews. So you might as well just sit down and relax. You're not going anywhere."

"You can settle over here with me," Selena offered. "There's plenty of room in this rocking chair for two."

A glare from Pepper silenced her.

The evening was filled with food, songs, jokes, laughing, teasing, and some serious moments of reflection. While the others played cards, Pepper sat in Tap's lap in the rocking chair by the fireplace.

She leaned her head against his chest. "It's been a nice evening."

Tap rocked back and forth for a while without speaking. Then he cleared his throat. "Well, Miss Pepper, the room isn't exactly filled with Colorado's most upstanding citizens. But they are our friends."

"They don't try to be someone they aren't."

"Nope. Cowboys and dance-hall girls, Indian lawyers and a shootist or two—that's who we are."

"How about ranchers?" she asked.

"Yeah . . . I hope I'll be allowed to be a rancher someday. But we're likely goin' to lose this place."

"I know." She put her arm around his shoulder and kissed his neck. "But we're in it together. And we're askin' the Lord to lead us. That's a whole lot more than we had six months ago."

"Six months ago I was wastin' my life away at the Arizona Territorial Prison."

"I don't even want to remember what I was doing," she admitted.

He stroked her blonde, wavy hair. "It's important for me to have something nice for you."

"It'll be tougher for you than for me. You know how little I've had in my whole life. Tap, I don't need very much."

"We'll have it someday, babe. If not here . . . well, the Lord must have something better for us." He laid his head on her hair.

Pepper knew there would be sadness in his big, brown eyes, so she refused to look at him.

"Are you all set for tomorrow?" she asked.

"I surely hope so."

"I brought your ruffled shirt with me. I can hardly wait to see you in it."

Tap hugged her tight and kissed the back of her neck.

"Careful down there!" Selena called. "You two haven't said those vows yet!"

Pepper turned and stuck out her tongue at all the others. She didn't let go of Tap.

"What time is everyone coming out?"

"The McCurleys and the others are going to leave before daylight. They plan on being here by eleven. The wedding will start at noon. The reverend says it won't take more than fifteen or twenty minutes. I figure we'll have dinner, and then they can all get on the road by two."

"That should put the whole passel back at McCurleys' by dark."

Pepper rocked the chair back and forth herself. "Can you imagine it, Mr. Tap Andrews? Tomorrow night we'll be sitting here by the fireplace—all alone."

"I don't aim to spend much time in the front room."

"Neither do I," she whispered. "How does your ear feel?"

"I seem to be hearin' everythin' fine."

"And your shoulder?"

"Can't lift my left arm above my head, and it itches like crazy. It'll heal."

"Tap . . . when you were hurtin', I told you some things . . . and now I don't know if you heard them. I've got to tell you before the wedding, or I'm goin' to regret it—"

He put his finger over her lips. "Shh! We aren't goin' to talk about the past."

Pepper felt tears well up in the corners of her eyes. "Tap, I really have to—"

"Now, look, Miss Pepper . . . I'm thick-headed and maybe slow, but I'm not dumb. I know a whole lot more than you think I know."

She sat straight up in his lap and looked him in the eyes.

"What do you know?"

"I know about a miscarriage. And regrets. And tough times. And dumb doctors who worry about you carrying babies . . . and all that."

"You do? You mean, you were listenin' out in the barn when I told you?"

"Yeah, and I was listenin' at that roadhouse corral with Dillard and Pardee."

"But you never said anything! You never responded. I—I thought . . . Why didn't you say something?"

"I guess I just didn't know what to say."

"Well, this is your last chance. What do you want to say?"

He put his hands on her cheeks and gently held her face in front of his. "I love you, Pepper Paige . . . and I'll try my best to make you a good husband."

She leaned over and kissed him on the lips.

"You mean, knowing that, you still want to marry me?"

"Lady, I'd marry you if you told me you had fifteen kids living in an adobe in Mexico."

"You would?"

"Yep." He kissed her on the cheek. "Eh . . . you don't, do you?"

"Have fifteen kids living in an adobe in Mexico?"

"Yeah."

"Nope." She giggled. "They're living in Tucson."

"It doesn't matter. You can't chase me off now!"

"You sure it doesn't matter?"

"You're the one, darlin'. Me and the Lord have already made up our minds."

Pepper laid her head back on his chest. They rocked back and forth in front of the fire for a very long time.

About midnight Tap, Wade, Wiley, and Stack hiked out to the barn carrying a dimly flickering lantern.

"Looks like the snow's lettin' up," Stack reported.

"That's good. Got to make sure the reverend and the others can get here tomorrow," Tap added.

"How many you figure will come out?"

"Oh . . . Pepper thinks about twenty all together, but I don't anticipate that many will want to brave the weather. Besides, we've got a houseful already."

After Tap fluffed up the fire in the tack room woodstove, the four stretched out in their bedrolls on the wooden floor. The smell of burning pine, the crackle of pitch, and the occasional yellow flash of fire flickering from the cracks in the stove danced across Tap's senses.

"You know, me and Pepper surely had a passel of dreams about how we were goin' to fix up this place. It's goin' to be hard to give 'em up." Tap sighed and rolled to his stomach. "Now if you boys promise not to tie me down, I think I'll get some sleep."

"We ain't promisin' nothin'!" Stack joshed. "So you jist better keep one eye awake all night."

As it turned out, Tap did sleep very little. But it had nothing to do with pranks from Stack and the others.

Lord, I don't really know what I'm doin' gettin' married now. I don't have anything to offer. She deserves better. Just a little cabin and a claim—at least I should have that much. Life on the drift is tough enough for a man—but for a lady? Of all women she needs some stability. I want it for her, Lord. I want it real bad.

Tap woke up with the fire already blazing. His toes and face were hot for the first time in several weeks.

"Well, boys, he's still here. I guess the weddin's on for today!" Wiley joked as he raised up on his elbow and watched Tap pull himself out of the bedroll.

"You ain't gettin' cold feet about this, are you?" Stack teased as he watched Tap rub his toes.

"I'm anxious to get this weddin' over. I can hardly wait until you three ride out of here, and I don't have to listen to this constant ribbin'."

"A little testy this mornin'," Wade joined in.

"I suppose it's nerves," Stack added. "Say, Wade, did you stew around like this before you and Rena got hitched?"

"Nope. I didn't have time."

"What do you mean?" Wiley asked.

"Well . . . me and Rena had been hittin' it off fairly good ever since Stack and Tap left us at the train station. Actually, we'd been hittin' it off *real* good. *¿Comprende?*" Wade raised his dark black bushy eyebrows. "So about a week ago we were walking down 16th Street in Denver, and I said, 'Maybe we ought to get married before we go down to Arizona.' And she said, 'Mr. Eagleman, are you asking me to marry you?'"

"And what did you say?" Wiley pressed.

"I just cleared my voice and said in a voice loud enough for everyone on the sidewalk to hear me, 'Why, yes, ma'am, I am. Miss Rena, will you marry me?'"

"What happened then?" Stack asked.

"Everybody around us clapped."

Tap tugged on his boots. "And what did she say?"

"She said, 'Mr. Eagleman, if you're serious, my answer is yes!' Well, I told her, 'Of course I'm serious.' Then she said, 'Prove it.'"

Wiley slipped his suspenders over his shoulders and straightened his britches. "Prove it?"

"That's what *I* said. 'What do you mean, prove it?' Then she said, 'There's the judge's office. Let's go get married right now.'"

"And what happened?" Wiley questioned.

"We did."

"Just like that?"

"Yep. It sure beats being nervous for a month."

"Nobody gets married just like that!" Wiley protested.

"Rena does."

Tap laughed and pulled on his coat. "Yep. She does have a knack for gettin' her way, doesn't she? Listen, boys, I'll go see that the fire's built in the house and that some coffee is boilin'."

To his surprise, the girls were stirring around. Rena gave Tap a pot of boiling coffee and a plate of sourdough biscuits and shoved him back out the door.

"You men will have to make a breakfast out of these. We don't have time for anything else! Until the wedding this house is off limits for you, Mr. Tap Andrews."

"But . . . I, eh . . ."

"Pepper said you already had your wedding clothes out in the barn, and she does expect you to shave. Would you please tell Mr. Eagleman to do the same?"

"Yeah, sure, but I . . ."

"Now go on, and quit muttering around!" Rena commanded as she scooted him out the door.

After breakfast Wiley rode out and checked on the cattle. Wade and Stack kept Tap company. He fed the horses, shoveled out the stalls, split some firewood, and filled the troughs with water from the well. Then he polished his boots, shined his spurs, brushed his store-bought coat, and stared at the ruffled shirt hanging beside it.

By 10:30 several guests had arrived, plowing through the snow. Not long afterwards, the McCurleys arrived with Reverend Houston.

"Those drifts are four feet in some places. It's going to be mighty hard gettin' back to the hotel," Bob McCurley projected.

"Well, I'm sure once we break open a trail, the others can follow in the tracks," Tap responded. "You know, Bob, I don't even know some of these folks."

"Pepper's made quite a few friends around the hotel."

"What time is it?"

"About eleven."

"I reckon it's time for me to dress up."

"Pepper said you are to come to the back door and stay in the kitchen until one of us comes and signals you out," McCurley instructed him.

"Right. The back door. I'll be over pretty soon."

Wiley and Wade left for the house. Stack was standing guard next to a bowl of hot water when Tap entered the tack room.

"Come on, you promised Pepper you'd shave."

"I don't know if I got time."

"You've got time!" Stack insisted.

Washing his face, neck, and hands, Tap shaved and began tugging on the ruffled shirt.

"I knew an old boy from New Orleans that wore a shirt like that once," Stack mused.

"Don't you start in on this shirt, Lowery!"

"He got shot for hidin' aces in the ruffles."

"That's enough!"

"You're right." Stack chuckled. "It looks darlin' on you."

"That's it. I'm not wearin' it!" Tap began to unbutton the shirt.

"Oh, no. You wouldn't want to break Pepper's heart now, would you?"

Tap pulled his Colt and waved it at the big piano player. "One more word out of you, and your shirt will have more holes than my hat!"

"Sorry, Andrews, but you can't wear the six-gun. Remember?"

"I'm wearin' my hat."

"Not while you say the vows."

"Well . . . I'll hold it then. Is my tie straight?"

"Yep. You look about as comfortable as a stuck pig ready to roast."

Stack and Tap walked over to the house. The snow was falling, more heavy and thick than before.

They slipped into the pantry and the kitchen from the back door. The room was stacked with steaming food and smelled of roast beef and apple pie.

Wiley peeked in at them. "Five minutes 'til doom. I mean, noon! Whewee! That's a nice shirt, Andrews."

"Be quiet, Wiley, or I'll tell Danni Mae you've got a wife and six kids livin' in Ogden!"

"A bit touchy, ain't he?"

"And nervous," Stack reported. "Look at the sweat roll down his collar."

Danni Mae shot into the room. "It's time! Come on, Stack, you've got to play the piano. We'll have to squeeze through the crowd."

"Don't these people have anything better to do?" Tap mumbled.

Danni Mae pulled Stack out of the kitchen. "Wiley, you stand at the door so I can signal you when it's Tap's turn to come out."

"Yes, ma'am. Do you think it's safe to leave him in the kitchen by himself?"

"If he knew how beautiful Pepper looks in that dress, he'd be runnin' to the altar right now."

"Pretty handsome, huh?" Tap asked.

"Andrews, you'll go weak in the knees, and we'll have to prop you up." Danni Mae laughed.

Suddenly they were all gone.

Tap heard the piano begin a slow waltz.

I answer "I will," and I say "I do." . . . After that I kiss the bride and slip the ring on her finger. . . . No, I give her the ring. Then I . . . the ring! It's in my saddlebag!

Tap charged out the back door. Spurs and jinglebobs rang as he sprinted across the yard.

I am not goin' to be late. I am not goin' to be late. . . . How long's that song anyway?

He shoved the barn door open wide. It crashed into a wooden pail of water that had been used for the horses. The contents washed across the dirt floor, but Tap leaped over the mud puddle and scampered into the tack room. He grabbed the purple velvet pouch, checked inside for the gold ring, and then shoved the whole thing into his vest pocket.

Rushing back across the barn, he caught a spur in the wire handle of the water pail and tried to free himself on the run. The pail bounced loose in front of his left foot. He stumbled and fell to the floor of the barn.

"No!" he cried out just as the ruffles slammed into the mud.

"I can't believe this! This really isn't happenin'. This is another bad dream, isn't it?"

He hurried back into the tack room and washed his hands in the shaving basin. Then he wet a towel and tried to sponge off the shirt. It only smeared the mud worse.

"I'll wear this other shirt. . . . I'll change . . . in the kitchen." He grabbed up the old shirt and ran back across the yard. Wiley and Wade hustled toward him.

"What happened to you?" Wade called out as they pulled him toward the back door.

"I went back for the ring."

"No, I mean what happened to your shirt?" All three men stepped into the kitchen.

"I, eh . . . slipped. I'll have to change."

"Don't have time, partner." Wiley held the door open.

"I've got time. Stack's still playing that waltz."

"It's his second time through. Pepper's beginnin' to panic."

"I've got to change."

"Not now. Go out there and look purdy. Maybe no one will notice," Wade insisted, pushing him out into the front room.

Everything became a blur, and Tap felt his face flush as someone shoved him up to the front of the room to stand beside Reverend Houston.

"Man, it's hot in here!" Tap whispered as he tugged at his collar.

Pepper stalked back and forth in the small bedroom, dragging the train of her beaded off-white wedding dress behind her.

"What do you mean, he's not out there?"

"Wiley saw him run out to the barn. He went to get him," Danni Mae reported.

"I knew it. I knew he'd find a way. He's either running away or going to be late! How many times has Stack played that song?"

"Just twice. Relax, girlie. You really are gettin' married."

"It's freezing in here! Can't you put some logs on the fire? My hands are almost frozen!"

"Really? It feels rather pleasant to me. You're just a bit nervous."

"I am not!" Pepper snapped. "It's time to get this started. We'll just have to go on."

"You can't start a weddin' without a groom."

A rap sounded at the door. Rena stuck her head inside. "Okay, you two. We've got a groom at the front of the room."

"How does he look?"

"Anxious . . . and, eh, rather muddy," Rena admitted. "But he's willing, girl. Now come on. It's your turn to shine!"

Did she say muddy?

Bob McCurley met her at the door, and she took his arm. While Stack pounded out a processional, Pepper and Mr. Mac serpentined through the crowd toward the fireplace. She saw Tap standing there—straight, strong, with a twinkle in his eyes, and the little-boy smile on his face.

He held his hat in front of him, covering the ruffles of his shirt.

She released Bob McCurley's arm and took Tap's. They turned to face Reverend Houston.

Danni Mae began to sing.

"You don't have to cover the ruffles now," she whispered. "No one can see them but me and the parson."

"Eh, they . . . sort of got messed up a tad," he confessed softly.

"What?" She reached up and pulled his hat down. "It—it looks like you rolled in the mud!"

"I tripped. I didn't mean . . . It's a fine shirt, but I didn't have time to change. Maybe you could have Danni Mae sing both her numbers, and I'll slip out to the kitchen. I've got another shirt in there, and I can—"

"You aren't going anywhere, buster—until you marry me!"

"Your hands are cold," he murmured.

"Yours are hot."

"I'm a little nervous."

"Me too."

When the song was over, Danni Mae and Stack moved through the crowd to the front and stood alongside Tap and Pepper.

"You're a mess, partner," Stack chided beneath his breath.

"So I hear."

After an opening prayer, Reverend Houston looked over the crowd and spoke in a deep, booming voice. "Forasmuch as these two persons have come hither to be made one in this holy estate, if there be any here present who knows any just cause why they may not lawfully be joined in marriage, I require him now to make it known or ever after to hold his peace."

Pepper glanced at Tap.

Then the front door burst open.

"I do! I object!"

They both spun around.

"Little Bob!" Pepper cried out. "What are you doing here? Go away!"

Waving his new rifle above his head, Little Bob Gundersen stomped into the room. "I object because I'm in love with Pepper, and I believe deep down in her heart she knows she loves me too!"

"I can't believe you'd do this to me, Little Bob!" Pepper cried.

Selena slid through the crowd and wrapped an arm around Little Bob's neck. Tap and Pepper saw her whisper something to him and then lean over and kiss him on the cheek.

"Eh, eh . . ." Little Bob turned bright red. "Uh, maybe I made a—a mistake! I might have acted rashly." He lowered the rifle. Selena brushed her lips against his. "Eh . . . go ahead. I'm kind of . . . I mean, I need to think this out."

Selena laced her long fingers into Little Bob's hand and tugged him toward the front door.

"I, uh, have no objections . . . your honor."

The two of them disappeared outside.

"That's why she wore a dress like that," Tap whispered.

"That's one reason," Pepper replied.

"Shall we continue?" Reverend Houston asked.

"Yes . . . please." Pepper nodded.

They did.

Right after they both repeated the vows, Tap leaned over to give Pepper a kiss.

"Not yet, cowboy. You don't get a kiss 'til I get my ring!" she announced.

The crowd roared.

When the service finally concluded, Tap was allowed to scoot to the kitchen and change his shirt. After that, there was food, laughter, music, dancing—and more food. Most of the time Pepper refused to let go of his arm. It was an arrangement he very much enjoyed.

Wade Eagleman finally pulled him aside. "Tap, have you looked out at that storm?"

"I suppose we should let folks get on the road home."

"I figure it's too late."

"Let me look!" Tap stepped out to the porch. The blast of frigid air felt refreshing, but the new snow had piled up almost another foot since daylight.

"They can't get out!"

"That's what I'm thinkin'."

Pepper slid up beside him. "It's cold out here, Mr. Andrews. What are you two doing?"

"Mrs. Andrews, no one will be goin' home in this storm. Looks like we'll be entertainin' guests."

"You mean they will . . . we can't . . . but I want to . . . That's not the way I planned it!"

"Well, come on. We might as well invite them to stay."

Tap pulled Pepper back into the front room and shouted to get everyone's attention. "Look . . . the storm's mighty rugged, and we figure you ought to stay with us 'til mornin'. Now we don't

have a lot of room, but you're welcome to stay by this fireplace
or up in the attic or in the kitchen by the woodstove, out in the
barn in the tack room, or up in the hayloft. But that bedroom
belongs to me and Pepper, and the first one that walks through
that door will be shot!"

Tap glanced down at Pepper's blushing face. "Is there anything
else you want to say about that, Mrs. Andrews?"

"Eh . . . no. I think they all get the picture."

The music and laughter blared once again as Tap pulled Pepper
over to the corner of the room.

"It will only be for one night," he assured her. "It'll likely clear
by mornin'."

It snowed heavily for three more days.

For a list of other books by
Stephen Bly
or information regarding speaking
engagements, write:

Stephen Bly
Winchester, Idaho 83555